ALTERNATIVE ZONING

A NOVEL

Rand Attaway

ISBN: 0615437338
ISBN-13: 9780615437330

CHAPTER ONE

As Mayor Leonard Grey closed the front door to his house on his way to work, he took pause to consider the day ahead of him and sighed. When he first assumed his mayoral duties, heading out to work the town constituency at seven in the morning was a matter of form, probably the character trait that had made him so popular for so long. Leonard was not as much of an institution as he was a welcomed tradition—but then, that was in better days. The village of Miller's Ferry was in a sad state, and as mayor, Leonard's days of accepting the credit for success had deteriorated into shouldering underserved blame for a barrage of present-day failings.

On his way out through the wrought-iron gate that bordered his tiny front lawn along Arch Street, a red minivan that had been parked about a block away started its engine and rolled toward Leonard as he rounded the front of his truck parked out on the street. As soon as he saw the van slow down, he knew it was no chance encounter; it was an unplanned, unwelcome meeting tossed onto his daily agenda.

As the vehicle rolled to a stop just abreast of him, its driver lowered the passenger window and leaned over to communicate her demands. "Good morning, Len," she stated.

"Good morning, Pam."

Pamela Holcum was considered a transplant by historic village standards, for she and her family had relocated from the nearby city of Cincinnati just ten years prior. After settling into her surroundings, she had experienced how outsiders could be treated when their opinion was not welcomed. Back then, she had taken to swallowing her pride and keeping her beliefs to herself in an effort to better fit in with the tight-knit community. However, the years of compromising her integrity had slowly chipped away at her moral fiber, until one night at a town hall meeting with the mayor, she used her allotted question time at the microphone to invite him and the rest of the village government to kiss her ass, an invitation that was declined. Since that point in time, she had continued through life without any further concern as to what others might think of her, and as result, she had experienced some of the best nights of sleep since moving to this remote outpost of civilization.

"Leonard, it's about Oak Street. When, exactly, are you planning to get it repaved?"

The effect of using his full first name was immediate. Only his mother had ever called him 'Leonard' in such a condescending tone, and that stopped once he turned twelve. "Pam, we've been through this before. The city manager is in charge of planning. He's the one you should be stalking."

"You know as well as I do, Len, that he won't so much as fart without getting your opinion first. Have you seen my street? Well, have you?"

"Listen Pamela—"

"A Goddamned pothole! That's what I park in. I noticed your street is nice and level. I sure as hell wish mine looked like this."

"I'm sorry, Pam, but you know there isn't enough money in the city budget for any capital improvements this year."

"I want disclosure, Len. I demand to see the books."

"Again, you need to go to the city manager's office for that. Now, if you don't mind, I have places to be."

"Don't think for one second I'm letting go of this. I'll get my street taken care of, one way or the other."

"I have no doubt about that at all, Mrs. Holcum," he said, returning the favor of the condescending tone.

Pamela mustered her most menacing look as she leaned back into her seat and rolled up the van window. For extra effect, she lingered slightly longer than necessary before slowly rolling away.

Leonard just shook his head and continued around to climb into his truck. As he sat behind the steering wheel, he replayed the conversation over in his head. Truly, the woman had turned into the bane of his existence, and he would love nothing more than to tell her how he really felt about her, but in his heart, he knew she was right. Many of the village streets had crumbled into ruin, a black reality of working within a budget that hadn't been out of the red in over three years.

Like any other catastrophe, the reasons behind their dire financial straits were many and varied. The State of Ohio was mired down in its own economic woes, leaving small communities like Miller's Ferry to fend for themselves in a hostile economy. This was no easy task, as individual wealth in the entire southwest corner of Ohio began to falter as well. Many of the established employers that had busily operated for decades around the extremities of Cincinnati had, over time, struggled to keep up with foreign trade, only to fail and whither into vague memories belonging to those who had once worked so hard to make these companies prosper. The job market had grown fiercely competitive as of late, resulting in wages and/or working hours everywhere being driven ever lower.

Leonard had remained relatively insulated from the financial hardships others contended with on a daily basis.

His career as chief editor of The Cincinnati Enquirer had out-lived both of his marriages, and three years to the day after publishing the news of the fall of the Twin Towers, Leonard holstered his pen for the last time and retired into the more sedate lifestyle within his lifelong home of Miller's Ferry, with the help of a generous pension.

The job of mayor was once a part-time passion, in addition to his full-time job in the city. In those days, it was an easy task, for the town practically ran itself. He was elected more on his popularity with the citizenry than for any political insight his worldview may have brought to the election—that and the simple fact that no one else wanted the job. Back in those days, his administration was known as the 'Grey Way.' Now, people quietly sang 'The old Grey Mayor just ain't what he used to be,' the final insult coming from Pamela Holcum's homemade sticker 'Old, Grey, and In The Way,' proudly displayed on the bumper of her minivan.

The truck struggled to start as he turned the key in the ig-nition. It was old for what it was, and like him, it had its good days and its bad days. The whine of the cranking engine slowed in its cadence, finally dwindling down to a stop for want of any electrical charge from its now-dead battery.

"Shit," he quietly complained to himself, not thrilled with the prospect of walking all day.

He left his truck in its shady parking spot on the street, to recover from whatever malady it was currently suffering, and began his trek towards the center of town. The walk was short—only four blocks—but at age sixty-nine, every step was starting to register in his body as two. There was a part of him that just wanted to blow off the day and go back inside his house. However, Leonard took his mayoral duties very serious-ly, and he was quite certain that if he were to go through a day without making his regular rounds, it would be registered as a sign of weakness.

Every city, town, village, and borough had what Leonard called 'pulse points.' When he had worked in Cincinnati, there were three diners he frequented where he found the real local cross-section of society, from lawyers and businessmen to factory and construction workers. After sharing meals with the patrons, he would return to his office and publish only what he knew to be in the majority's heart. Through this talent, he acquired an uncanny ability to sell newspapers, predict elections, advise city officials, and champion only the issues about which the city really cared. The year after he retired from the newspaper, circulation fell by 9 percent; he always felt it was undoubtedly a direct result of his absence, not the coming of the age of electronic media, as other would explain.

Miller's Ferry had three critical pulse points: the Ferry Landing Café, Richard's Barber Shop, and Itchy's Pool Hall. Before going to his office in town, he started his day by paying a visit to one or more of these establishments to better ascertain what was at the forefront of the villagers' minds. Each of these businesses had been a common meeting ground of various segments of the community since they had first been licensed to open, and as a regular in all of them, he had been granted the coveted status of 'One with an opinion that matters.'

Working the public like this was something that had served him well during all of his years as mayor. He had accomplished more good for the village while networking in the café over coffee, finding out what 'the real deal' was down at the pool hall, or listening to the laments that had been unburdened in the barber shop than he ever had within the walls of his official office. The day before, he had spent the entire morning at Richard's, so to satisfy his current delicate condition, he made his way over to the closest pulse point, The Ferry Landing.

The Pissquatta River had never been, nor would it ever be a navigable waterway. While the Midwest prospered and grew amidst the arteries that comprised the Erie Canal System, the Pissquatta had never managed to be anything to anyone other than an inconvenience; even the Indians who first occupied this land did not have a name for the waterway that was only three feet at its deepest point. It was christened 'Pissquatta' by founding father Heinrich Putzkammer, the advance-man of a group of German settlers bound from Pennsylvania. It was a name he was pretty certain belonged to a local tribe of Indians, although no record of their existence has ever been found. He said it with such authority, however, that anyone who listened to him was quite convinced he had to be right, and out of early common usage, the Pissquatta River carried its new name from the head waters seven miles to the north of the newly incorporated village of the same name, down to the Ohio River three miles south.

Heinrich liked the lay of the lightly forested land and envisioned a future burgeoning metropolis that would eventual swallow up the already established Cincinnati. So certain was he of their bright future that he laid the town out on the west side of the river so that Cincinnati would be obliged to build the eventual bridge to connect the two cities. "All roads," he often boasted, "will one day lead to Pissquatta."

The early days of Pissquatta were dream-filled pursuits of greatness that, in time, ended in profound mediocrity. Much of the forest was cleared for agriculture, and the bounty of grains and corn was ultimately fed to Pissquatta's first established business, the Grain Mill alongside the river. Everything built within the fledgling community was for the sole benefit of the community, except for the mill, with end customers as far away as Cincinnati.

Idea after idea failed to bring stature to the little community. The fledgling Lutheran college folded after only five years, due to lack of enrollment. The nomination for state capital was never even considered by the rest of the state simply because of its funny-sounding name, and the canal project to the Ohio River was abandoned due to lack of interest after only 500 yards had been dug. In the end, the only businesses to enjoy even a modicum of success were the farmers and the mill.

The miller, in an effort to shorten his wagon ride to all points east, built a makeshift ferry out of a large raft and a heavy rope that stretched across the slow-moving river. Eventually, others within the village rose to the responsibility of managing the ferry service on a full-time basis, until the two-lane bridge that connected Pissquatta with the rest of the world was built in 1928. By this time, the village had grown weary over the snickering they endured from the rest of the state as the 'Piss Squatters,' so with the christening of the new bridge, they also rechristened their town in memory of the original Miller's Ferry.

Throughout the rest of the century, Miller's Ferry remained a modest little farm community. As the city of Cincinnati broadened its reach, the little community became a bedroom community for urban workers searching for a quiet respite.

Although opinion differs as to where the Ferry Landing really was, the café of the same name treasured its memory at its own location within the heart of town, a good quarter mile away from the river. It was open for business every day of the week at five thirty in the morning. Its walls were adorned with old photographs and paintings of river ferries, none of which were the original Miller's Ferry. No one seemed to mind this simple fact, however, and visitors would often look at the walls and wax nostalgic at how blissfully simple things must have been in those days.

The café was divided into two dining areas, with a counter and booths in the original section of the building and a dining room for tables and chairs in the addition that had been built several years after opening. The counter was usually occupied by diners trying to catch a hearty breakfast rich in fat and cholesterol before their morning commute into the city. The booths, on the other hand, were mostly filled with old friends or retired couples desiring to see and be seen in the town's hottest breakfast nook.

The adjoining dining room was where the real action lay. Tables that had been set up individually around the room would eventually migrate together in clusters, as islands unto themselves, for the social strata of the village. The occupants of each enclave were comprised of representatives of the different facets of Miller's Ferry citizenry. In the corner could usually be found senior members of the United Methodist Church, while just a short toast crust toss away could found an equal number of Lutherans. The Baptists, Pentecostals, and Catholics generally congregated in small outbreaks of tables or in some of the booths for lack of a vacant table.

The most noteworthy of tables was to be found basking in the sun before the lace-curtained windows that looked out onto Sycamore Street. This regal setting, worthy of the company at the Last Supper, was filled with the elite members of the community that held the deepest historical roots within Miller's Ferry. To sit at this table, one needed not only to live within the Historic District, but they also had to be a namesake of one of the original settlers. This was the ruling post of the town's old guard (the youngest diner being sixty-seven) and the sole collective of the 'opinion that matters most.'

Leonard made his entrance into the main part of the café and worked his way along the occupants of the counter and the booths that flanked his transit through the restaurant, shaking hands, asking about their lives, and feigning interest in their responses. There was once a time when he'd walk into the room, everyone would call out to him and beg him to join them for coffee, but now his people paid little attention to him, and fishing for salutations was becoming a more commonplace task.

As he made his way into the attached dining room, his reception became a little warmer. The Methodists greeted him warmly as he approached their table and asked if he would not mind filling in for the vacationing Liturgist during the next Sunday service. As a member of that particular congregation, it was a job he performed often and was well received for his engaging oratory skills. His particular passion was for any reading from the Old Testament, which he more than adequately performed with an appropriate balance of fervor and severity.

At the Lutheran table, they asked if he might say a few words during the dedication ceremony of the new weather vane to be placed atop their steeple, which was proudly the tallest point in town. Always happy to stay in tight with this church, he warmly accepted their invitation.

After chatting briefly with the other denominations, Leonard turned his attention to the largest collection of tables. This group had no formal title, but they had met for coffee and/ or breakfast every weekday morning for the past decade. Rising to greet him first was Beatrice Schimmel, who was in charge of the village Historical Society. She and the committee of three who were her charge always sat with their backs to the window, facing the rest of the dining room. The Historical Society had traditionally wielded much authority in the older section of town, where the appearances and upkeep of the old houses were concerned. No improvements to the structures could be made without their express authorization. Until a final and successful challenge to their authority had stripped them of their influence, they had often used their authority to leverage home owners into complying with other agendas in town that they personally favored.

"Morning Len," Beatrice said with a warm smile.

"Bea, you're looking as beautiful as ever."

"You silver-tongued devil. Get your butt over here and sit next to me," she continued with a girlish chuckle.

Leonard caught the attention of a nearby waitress who was busily bussing a table across the room and motioned for a cup of coffee to be brought over. This was more of a formality, for she often preempted his cryptic signaling with a fresh cup at the ready.

"How is everybody today?" he asked, taking the empty seat next to Beatrice.

"Fine, Len, fine," replied Ernest Hoffler, owner of the town's largest insurance company. "We were just talking about you."

"So that's why my ears were burning. All good, I hope."

"We were just wondering what is on the agenda for the town hall meeting next week."

"Nothing new Ernie—mostly just budget and finance."

"That should be a short meeting then," interrupted Robert Hoffler, Ernie's older brother and partner in the firm.

"Sure, Bob. It will most likely be a short one," responded Leonard, slightly annoyed.

The rest of the table fell into an awkward silence over Robert's faux pas. He knew they all condemned him for saying what the rest of them felt, but at eighty-two years old, he apologized for nothing.

"I don't have to tell you all how bad things are getting. We're broke, without any real hope coming down the road in the foreseeable future. Jenny, tell them what you told me yesterday."

Jenny Kirchofer was finance director for Miller's Ferry. Although she had been a longtime attendant of the group's morning sojourns, she rarely initiated a conversation and limited her shy answers to brief statements of fact. "A lot of people aren't paying their village taxes," she said.

"People aren't paying their taxes, huh? Why do you think that is?"

"Because they're all a bunch of lowlife deadbeats living out in the developments, that's why," replied Robert angrily. "They're not a real part of this town, so why should they feel any sense of loyalty?"

"I'm sorry, Bob, but I have to disagree. I've seen the names on the list, and a lot of them have lived in this town their whole lives. I know money has become tight for some folks out there, but the bottom line is they don't trust the village government to manage their tax money in the town's best interest. They don't see any improvements being made, so they're left to wonder what the point in it all is."

"It's worse than that, Len," added Jerald Brauer, former owner of Brauer Real Estate. "My son has over a dozen meetings scheduled this week with people putting their houses on the market. Some of them are even in the Historic District." This last revelation was met with concerned gasps erupting from around the table.

"I'm sorry folks. I can't help but think this whole thing is only going to get worse before it gets better. Let's face it… we just don't have what it to takes to make new families want to move here anymore, and we really need that new blood if we are going to grow and survive."

With this, all eyes turned to the four occupying the far end of the table. Their names were all Drescher, but individual lineage had gone back too far without any common connections to determine where in time they might actually be related. The 'Drescher Four,' as they had come to be known, comprised the bulk of the village Planning Commission.

It was through their committee that ideas were born to draw the outside world into their little community. This challenging course of action was something the town had endeavored to do since their inception, with little in way of tangible results. In the end, they relied heavily on their small-town charm to be the ultimate draw.

Tom Drescher, leader of the four, cleared his throat and rose to make the official statement. "We are continually looking into new ideas, with the intent of increasing foot traffic in the downtown area throughout the year. We're very excited about some planned events this summer, which we really feel should start bringing in more people to support the businesses on Main Street."

"Like what?" asked Robert, more an accusation than an inquiry.

"Well, we're going to do the Drive-Ins again, every third Saturday this time."

The bulk of the table groaned in response to the thought of more Drive-Ins. It was a well-intentioned idea a few years back, conceived by a local classic car club in town, to provide a venue by which they could better showcase their town. By closing off the streets and lining up collectors' cars, along with food stands manned by the various religious denominations of the village, it was believed this would be catalyst enough to draw in car enthusiasts from all over. As it turned out, it was an idea utilized by virtually every other village of their size, diluting the potential draw to a localized regional few who had no intention of leaving their own sleepy little towns in favor of this one.

"Is that it, another shameless self-promotion for the car club?"

"Well, like I said, Bob, we're looking into lots of stuff. A suggestion was raised about starting a Soap Box Derby League here. There are towns that get a big draw for those kinds of things."

"Where are you planning on staging the event, Tom?" asked Leonard.

"Right here in town, I guess."

"We live at the bottom of a large river valley. You have to go three or four miles out of town before you find the first hill to send them down."

"Well, we haven't quite worked out the details yet."

"You have anything else, Tom?"

"I was going to wait until the meeting to announce it, but this year we will be holding our first annual Miller's Ferry ten-K run. We anticipate a lot of folks coming in from Cincinnati for that one."

"That's good, everyone, really good. Thank you, Tom," replied Leonard, inviting the standing Drescher to sit back down with the remaining three.

"The Planning Commission is coming up with some ideas here, folks, but everyone is invited to offer up a solution. The plain and simple truth is that our way of life is dying, and it is up to us to do something about it." What was to follow was Leonard's specialty: a civic call to duty. President Kennedy may have asked America first what it could for its country, but he had never achieved the level of zeal that Mayor Grey could inspire. "I hold the highest office in this town, but you are the ones who will really lead us all into the new century. Whether we succeed or fail will be determined by the actions we take here and now. We're on our own, folks. The State has forgotten all about us, and even our own people are starting to turn their backs, refusing to pitch in with their taxes. When the foundation of society begins to crumble, as it admittedly is right now, it will require a steady resolve from a stalwart few to shore it back up. Look around the table, everyone, and behold the future heroes of Miller's Ferry."

The effect was predictably immediate, and had they been drinking anything other than coffee, there may have been high toasts all around. Beatrice sat at least three inches taller in her chair, with the other members of the Historical Society following her lead. The Hoffler brothers nodded in sage agreement while stroking their chins, and the Dresher Four heaved a sigh of relief once the burden of ensuring the future of the town had been seemingly lifted from their exclusive shoulders.

Satisfied that his work there was complete, Leonard nodded to the waitress for the check. "Well, you folks carry on your good work here. As for me, I have a city to run." Leonard politely took the check from the waitress and walked heroically through the dining room and out to the cash register at the front of the restaurant.

After leaving the Ferry Landing to the imagined choruses of "Battle Hymn of the Republic," Leonard returned to a more natural posture and a slower gait on the way to his office two blocks away. As dissent grew within the town, and with no money left for damage control, all he had left were his words of inspiration. He knew he had left many of the morning diners with a renewed sense of purpose, but this was not going to sustain Miller's Ferry for much longer, regardless of how heroic everyone felt.

Outside of the town was farmland ready to be subdivided into new neighborhoods. The meager excuse for a shopping center on the way into town had already applied for zoning on their next expansion. Plans had been drawn up to make better use of their sewer and water systems, and the architectural drawings for the new high school were nearly completed. Everything was ready for a town on the move; all it lacked were the new people and a broader tax base to make it happen.

CHAPTER TWO

Leonard turned off the lights to his office and closed the door behind him on his way out.

In the outer office, Chuck Bosner was emptying his assistant's trashcan into the larger bin of his janitor's cart. "Hey there, Mr. Grey! You workin' late?"

"I'm not working late, Chuck. I'm hiding."

"Oh? From who?"

"The world."

"That's a tough one."

"You can't even imagine. Goodnight, Chuck."

"'Night, sir."

As Leonard walked out onto the street, the sun was all but set. All that was left of the day were the last remnants of light fading behind the neighborhood tree line to the west.

"Evening, Mayor!" called out one of the firemen who was sitting outside the open bay doors of the attached fire department.

"Hey, Larry. How did that last call turn out?"

"Car wreck out on County Line."

"Hmm. Happy ending?"

"Not for the passenger, I'm afraid."

"Sorry to hear that."

"Made the new kid puke."

"Not a total loss then."

"Wish I could agree with you, Len, but I had twenty bucks that said he'd make it to the end of the month."

"Just when you think you've got the human race all figured out, someone has to go and prove you wrong, eh?"

"Don't rub it in."

"'Night, Larry."

"'Night, Mayor."

Larry Drescher (no relation to the Drescher Four) had been the village fire chief longer than Leonard had been mayor. He knew a lot about public service but little of public accountability, at least nothing like Leonard's office endured. Larry sympathized with the hard knocks Leonard had been taking as of late, but he secretly felt relieved that, by the grace of God, he did not go.

As Leonard walked down the street in the direction of his home and his sick truck, a healthy Volvo coming down the other side of the street slowed to a stop. There was a hum as the window rolled down.

"Evening, Len. Couldn't help but notice your truck didn't go to work with you this morning. Need a lift?"

"Thanks, Mike," he responded, crossing the street.

Mike Pennington had been his best friend and neighbor since Leonard bought his house over thirty years ago.

"Is this a chance encounter, Mike, or are you stalking me?" asked Leonard, stepping into the car.

"Definitely a stalk."

Mike accelerated to the posted speed limit of twenty-five and rounded the corner to their respective homes.

"I've been stalked by better than you."

"Yeah, I saw Pamela talking to you this morning," replied Mike. "She is something else."

"That woman is like a pit bull. She just never lets go. Sometimes I just don't know why I put up with all of this."

"You know what they say. Heavy lies the head that wears the crown."

"I'm serious, Mike. I don't think I can fix this village anymore. It might be time to hang it up."

Mike pulled the Volvo into its parking spot behind his house and shut off the engine. "Come on in and have a beer, Len. You sound like you need somebody to talk you off a ledge."

"Promise we won't talk about the town?"

"Promise."

"What am I going to do about this town, Mike?"

"You know what you need, Len?"

"No, what?"

"A brilliant idea," replied Mike, coming back from the kitchen with two open beers.

"Last I checked, I was all out of those."

"Oh, a good idea's out there, Len. You just haven't found it yet. Here," he said, handing him some liquid inspiration.

"Thanks," Leonard replied before tilting it back for a long, welcomed gulp. "Oh that's good. Hey, here's an idea… we throw a giant kegger in the park and charge $10,000 a head."

"Hmm… although the idea has merit, I fear only two people in the county could afford the cover charge."

"Alright then, so we charge ten bucks a head to cover our costs, everyone shows up, and we all get good and drunk as we watch everything go down the shitter." Leonard took another drink and put the bottle down onto the coffee table in front of him.

Mike leaned forward in his chair and slipped a coaster under the offensive sweating bottle.

"I love this town, and I'm having a lot of trouble watching it die," admitted the mayor.

"You know, Len, I didn't move here until after I made tenure at the university. I'll never have the connection with it that you do, but I have to admit that I fell in love too. The place is pretty as picture, lousy with charm, and about as friendly as it gets. Hell, the town practically sells itself. So why don't more people want to live here?"

"Ohio is lousy with pretty, charming, and friendly towns. It's what we do best. I think people pick towns the same way they pick cars, like there's some kind of feature or accessory that resonates with them and draws them in. I just don't know what our accessory is here."

"That's a philosophical concept I could have used when I was still teaching—the Zen of town and car shopping."

"You must have been some kind of groovy teacher in your day."

"You ain't kidding, Len. Do you know how I spent my first sabbatical?"

"I'm sure you're going to tell me," he replied, reaching for his beer.

"I went in search of Al Ginsberg by hitchhiking across the Southwest."

"You're kidding! How Kerouac."

"Precisely."

"Did you find him?"

"Oh yeah. After four months of hitching 1,500 miles of highway, interacting with over 300 people, being stung by a couple of scorpions, and emptying over 100 pounds of sand and gravel from my shoes, I finally found him hanging out in a ramshackle, tin-roofed hovel on an Indian reservation. As it turns out, he was on a sabbatical as well."

"Really? What did you do when you found him?"

"Ate peyote and read poetry."

"And what did you get from all of this… uh, enlightenment?"

"To be honest, I got sick. Turns out I didn't have the stomach for peyote."

"To better days my friend," suggested Leonard, holding his bottle up in a mock toast.

Mike reciprocated and tilted back his bottle.

"So Mike, now that you have officially started your retirement, what do you have planned next?"

"I think I'll run for mayor."

"Oh, if you want my office, I'll give it to you."

"No thanks. I don't need that kind of stress." Mike took another drink of his bottle and reconsidered the question. "When I began teaching, I thought I'd wait to see where my career took me and just go with the flow. When I made professor, I figured I'd work there until they had to drag me from that school kicking and screaming. When I was awarded my chair, I suddenly felt like I had gone as far as I could, and I started to wonder, What's the point? I could work another ten or fifteen years, but my heart just wouldn't be in it anymore. Philosophy is a mandatory elective students must endure but will never embrace. I have been a wandering Socrates looking for my Plato, but in the end, I was nothing more than a punch line."

"I'm sorry. I had no idea you felt that way."

"Oh, it's not your burden, my friend, and I don't intend to make it mine any longer. The world is my oyster, and after cleaning out the last of my office today, I shall commence on an exploration of everything."

"That's a pretty lofty goal."

"It's more than that. It's a responsibility."

"Let me know how that works out for you."

"I'll guarantee you daily reports over something cold and wet."

"Just let me know if your so-called 'explorations' find a way to turn this town around. Cheers."

After receiving a jumpstart the next morning from the now
retired Professor Pennington, Leonard's truck carried him out
onto the town to start his rounds. He refused to think of the
rusting hulk that was his truck as old, rather as classic. His
other neighbors quietly mumbled at how its appearance on the
street out front lowered their real estate value, but he could no
more get rid of it than cut off his right arm.

He and the truck had known better days, like the first day
he drove it off the lot in downtown Cincinnati or the day he
ran the picture of enthusiastic Germans hammering away at
what was left of the Berlin wall on his front page. They had
accompanied one another through hard times, like the first
time the odometer ran past the 100,000 mile mark or the hor-
rific destruction in New York City. It had carried him to his
two weddings and the many subsequent court appearances that
ended them. His truck was his Deacon's Masterpiece, and he
was determined to see his old friend outlive him in the end.

They pulled up outside of Itchy's around nine o'clock, when
he officially opened for business. Itchy's Pool Hall had become
an established part of the town culture, just a mere six months
after first opening its doors fifteen years earlier. During the day,
the old men who designated themselves the keepers of the town
wisdom congregated around scarred tables playing cards and
dominoes or simply recounting days of glory, the days of fishing
on the Ohio River. At night, it became the domain of a younger
crowd, each member eager to prove his mettle on the green felt
field of battle. Reputations were made and lost every night as
money passed from one wallet to another.

Leonard followed three young teenagers into the parlor,
curious as to why they might be there instead of school. They
lingered at the entrance, testing the waters they were about to
enter. With no one between them and any of the tables, they

ventured deeper into the dim interior and mustered around the table furthest from the door and any prying eyes that happened by on the street outside. The leader of this group fished some quarters out of his pocket and placed them into the coin mechanism mounted on the side of the table, plunging the lever in to render the satisfying sound of fifteen heavy balls traveling through the interior of the table and spilling out into a collection point at the end. As he assembled the balls onto the table for a game, an older man with one arm wondered into the hall from a room in the back.

"Ah! Here to play a little eight-ball, huh?" he said to the leader of the young trio.

"That's right."

"Why aren't you kids in school?"

"Thought we'd take a day off."

"Hmm, I see. You fellas any good?"

"Yes, sir," he replied with mounting confidence.

"If you want to play in my hall, you have to play me first. How much money y'all got?"

Unprepared for this question, the three joined in a huddle to confer and sorted through the money in their wallets.

"We got thirty-seven," replied their emboldened leader.

"That's a good thing, 'cause it costs exactly thirty-seven dollars a game to play me."

The leader put the money on the rail of the table and smiled. "You ain't got but one arm. Hardly seems fair, but we'll gladly take your money."

"That's mighty big of you, son. You wanna break?"

"Sure," he replied with a shrug, taking a cue from its rack on the wall and setting up for his first shot. His friends lined the wall behind him, smiling as they recollected the pool-playing prowess he had frequently demonstrated in his dad's paneled basement.

His opening shot sent a resounding thwack echoing about the parlor walls, scattering the balls nicely, but sinking none.

The one-armed man selected a worn pool cue with a pronounced warped bow in it. After assessing all potential shots, he laid the unlikely stick on the table and sent the cue ball off the opposing rail and into the three-ball, delivering it neatly to the corner pocket. Shifting only a foot to his left, he did the same for the one-ball and three more balls before missing a particularly challenging shot off three cushions.

The rattled youth stepped up to the table, visibly shaken by the one-armed man's performance. He picked the one shot he knew he could not miss, regardless of how it might set him up for the next shot; he just wanted to get anything off the table. He lined up his stick for a straight linear shot on a ball only five inches from the pocket and blew it as result of unintentional deflection. The cue ball careened off in a direction that connected with the eight-ball, sending it perilously toward a side pocket. He held his breath as he watched the potential scratch shot roll all the way up the edge of the pocket and stop.

"Hmm. That's an interesting strategy, son. Okay, let's wrap this up. Two-ball in the corner." Thwack! The cue ball travelled obediently across the felt and performed his bidding, rolling to stop in front of next shot. "Seven in the side." Thwack! "And the eight... aw, you know where." As the eight-ball fell into the pocket, the one-armed man picked up their lawn-mowing and leftover lunch money and put the folded wad of ones and fives into his shirt pocket. "Well, son, you're out of money and any other reason to be in my pool hall. Now, do us both a favor and get your ass back to school so you can learn something worthwhile, because you ain't never gonna make a living at this game if you can't even beat a one-armed man."

Broke and defeated, the three shuffled out of the pool hall single file, dragging their deflated egos on the ground behind them.

Leonard chuckled at the spectacle. "Oh, there's trouble right here in River City..." he started.

"...And I mean with a capital T, that rhymes with P, which stands for Poooool. Hiya, Len. Ain't seen you here in a spell."

"Morning, Itchy."

Like Leonard, James 'Itchy' Jackson was from Miller's Ferry and always would be. He had spent much of his life working the western rivers, building tows out of the many cargo barges that travelled America's river infrastructure. It was a career he loved and lived until a mishap with a failed wire coupling separated his left arm from the rest of his body. The nickname 'Itchy' had been awarded by his shipmates after he returned to the boat from an unfortunate night in the bed of a hooker in Memphis. Whenever asked of the source to his name, he simply replied, "Don't ask."

With a generous settlement from his old employer, Itchy returned to Miller's Ferry and opened up the Pool Hall that bore his name. Since that time, Itchy arose to occupy an important niche within the village hierarchy through his clientele. For men like Leonard, it was valuable exposure to the citizenry who lived across the tracks from the morning diners at the Ferry Landing.

"So tell me, Itchy, what was your goal was just now. Were you re-aligning that boy's moral compass or just after his money?"

"Does it matter?"

"No, I don't suppose it does."

"I just put on a fresh pot of coffee, Len. Buy you a cup?"

"Sure," replied Leonard and then fell in behind Itchy to the back office. "The hall's a little dead today, Itch. The new economy hitting you as well?"

"Nope. The fellas are up at the cemetery this morning."

"Oh, that's right. They're burying Ned Bateman today." Leonard inwardly admonished himself for forgetting an occasion where he could inspire and network. Ned Bateman had died while holding the office of the worshipful master at the local Masonic lodge and would undoubtedly draw a large crowd.

"Take a load off, Len," said Itchy, motioning to the old vinyl couch, visibly adorned with makeshift duck tape patches. "Is it too early for a snort?" he asked, holding up a pint of Kentucky's Finest straight bourbon.

"Not at all. In fact, why don't you put the pot back on the burner? No sense polluting good whiskey."

"That's what I like about you, Len. You're damn good company, no matter what company you're in. Here," he said, passing the half-filled coffee cup of liquor and then taking a seat behind an old wooden desk cluttered with invoices, receipts, and candy wrappers. He leaned back in the equally old matching oak desk chair and put his feet up onto the edge of the desk that had a shallow indentation, worn from bearing years of resting boot heels. Hanging on the wall behind him was proudly displayed a trophy plaque: Mounted on polished mahogany were the remnants of a broken pool cue, suspended above a small brass plate that read 'Lloyd's Tavern, 1967 Bar Fight; My First, His Last.'

"The 'new economy'? is that what they're calling it?"

"I suppose. It sounds more like an effort to put a sprig of parsley on a turd sandwich. It doesn't matter what you call it, it's still hard to stomach."

"Ha, ha," chuckled Itchy. "You have a unique outlook, Mr. Mayor, especially when you consider you're the one that has to serve this turd sandwich of a town."

"How did we get here, Itchy? How did everything get so bad so quick?"

"I suppose that one should be asked of better minds than mine, but if I had to speculate, I'd say our country has been riding a freight train that for some time now has been building speed on its way down the tracks. Hell, we've been so fired up about the ride that we didn't have enough sense to look down the tracks at the bridge that was out. Now we're riding that ol' train right on down into the gorge."

"You're the one with a unique outlook."

"Yeah, you can put that one in a fortune cookie if you want, but it's just an observation. We can't do nothin' to fix the past, my friend. All we can do is try to put the shattered pieces of this ol' wreck back together and get 'er back on the tracks. That'll definitely take better a mind than mine... like say, yours. What're your plans on gettin' our freight train runnin' again, Len?"

"Same thing we've been trying to do since 1802—make this the kind of town people will want to move to and settle down in."

"That ain't been working out so good now, has it?"

"You have a way of stating the obvious, Itch. No, we haven't, but then we just haven't found our draw yet. There's no sense in jumping on the soapbox if I don't have anything to bark over."

"Hmm. What you need is a hook, and that'll have to be something nobody else 'round here's got. It's too late for textile or heavy industry, nothing to quarry, no real opportunity in farming. You know, I've been thinking of putting in a snooker table, just to see if it catches on."

"I can't say I've ever played snooker or straight billiards. In fact, I can't say I've ever seen anybody offer it anywhere either. You might be on to something, Itchy."

"Well, there you go. If that don't bring 'em running into town, I don't know what will."

"It's certainly a start, Itch. The fact is, I think we've been holding onto our hillbillyism for too long. I talked to Starbucks about what it would take to get a franchise in our town, and you know what they told me?"

"No, what?"

"They said there aren't any people in Miller's Ferry civilized enough to pay three bucks for a cup of coffee."

"Hmm. Well. Now that's being mean spirited of them. I'd say we're plenty civilized enough to spend too much money on overpriced coffee."

"I don't think a Starbucks would bring them running in, but it might make a difference to someone from the city looking for a place outside the limits… you know, something familiar to their original environment."

"I see your point, Len. What we lack is dazzle."

"That and a hook you can't get anywhere else in this part of the state."

"I'm sure something will come to you."

"Yeah, I can only hope, but it's going to take more than one man coming up with an idea." Leonard was winding up for another tree-stump moment. "It's going to take the whole damn village, Itchy. It's going to take a new snooker table or a movie theatre that's open more than two nights a week. It's going to take a real Italian restaurant, maybe a trendy café and bookstore. It's going to take a town that is willing to shake off the dust of a routine it has been choking on for far too long. Thinking outside of the box has to be our mantra if we are ever going to bring in new blood and breathe some life back into this tired old village."

"How 'bout that. 'Nother shot, Mayor?"

"Sure, Itchy." Leonard held his cup out for a refill and then sat back in the couch again. "I know I go over the top sometimes…"

To this statement, Itchy raised a single eyebrow while he topped off his own cup.

"Okay, a lot, but we have to start rethinking the way people view Miller's Ferry. This town has so much potential, and it really must be a collective effort if we are going to make any headway."

"You've inspired me, Leonard—or maybe it was you and the early Kentucky's Finest—but whatever the case, I'm going to order that snooker table. Hell, I might even change the name to 'Itchy's Billiard Parlor,' maybe give the place a real Victorian feel."

"Now you're talkin', brother."

"I can see where you're coming from, Len. Traditionally, people have been born and raised and made families of their own right here in this same little town. These past ten years, though, I have watched as more and more of the kids move away. Hell, that little pool shark I beat this morning probably has no intention of staying here one minute longer than he has to."

Leonard sighed. "There's no helping it, Itch. It's hard to compete with the Ferraris of the modern world when all this town has to offer is an old Ford."

"Not old, my friend. Classic."

"Amen! Nonetheless, we're losing more than we're holding onto. What moves away will have to be replaced. If new blood is the only way to ensure the future of Miller's Ferry's, I doubt what this town has been will still be around fifty years from now."

"Then shame on us, Mayor. Shame on us."

As Leonard stepped from his truck in front of his house, he noticed an attractive young woman walking down the sidewalk, holding a spiral notebook. It was Amanda Bremner, a member of his church, with a fine family of a husband and three kids living in the new development.

"Evening, Mayor," Amanda called out smiling, still fifty feet away and closing.

"Well hello there, Amanda. What brings you to this neck of the woods?"

"I'm here to see Mr. Pennington," she replied as she arrived at his neighbor's gate.

"And in what kind of plan has that scoundrel enlisted you?"

"Mr. Pennington is helping out with a project of mine. I'm writing a book."

"Really? What about?"

"The houses here in Miller's Ferry. It's going to be called Haunted Miller's Ferry. I'm cataloging and writing about the hauntings in some of the houses around town."

"I had no idea there were any."

"I've found six so far. How about your place? Have you ever experienced any strange sounds, any bumps in the night?"

"No, Amanda, can't say I have. How far into it are you?"

"It's mostly notes, but I have the first few chapters hammered out."

"I'm proud of you, Amanda. Let me know when you're ready to have your first copy proofed. I'd love to help out."

"Thanks, Mr. Grey! I'll do that. Well, have a good night."

Amanda passed through the gate and met Mike Pennington at his front door.

"Evening, Mike!" Leonard called out from the street.

"Evening, Leonard. Have you found inspiration yet?"

"I'm getting there."

"Good. Let me know if you need any help. Goodnight, Mr. Mayor."

"Good night, Professor."

Leonard walked through his own gate and looked back to his neighbor's house. The two chatted briefly at the door and then disappeared inside. Leonard considered the future welcome sign at the edge of town: 'Welcome to Miller's Ferry, Home of Award-Winning Author Amanda Bremner.' Something like that might bring them running, he envisaged. Nah.

CHAPTER THREE

As Leonard pushed the mower across the modicum of grass in his front yard, he reflected on the sermon Pastor Cheryl had just delivered two hours prior. Like the town, the numbers in her congregation were slowly ebbing away. Upon her arrival to the modest Methodist church only five years earlier, the pews had been quite full, and the response to her services had been enthusiastic. She knew the troubles families were facing and that her services were not to blame for the diminished attendance, but she was at a loss as how to remedy the problem. In the confidence of people like Leonard, she conveyed a deep desire to make the kind of difference that would fill the pews again, and like Leonard, she was on the lookout for a good idea to make that happen.

As his mower finished devouring the last tufts of grass, Leonard surveyed the lawn one last time before shutting the sputtering machine down. The minimal exertion was not enough to even break a decent sweat, but still he ran the back of his hand across his brow to signify the conclusion of his weekly outdoor chores.

"You look like you could use something tall and cold," came a voice from the yard behind him.

Leonard turned around and grinned. "Sure, Mike. You buying?"

"C'mon, old man. Let's get out of this hot sun."

After Leonard finished putting the mower away in its shed around back, he crossed over into his neighbor's yard and entered through the rear door into the kitchen.

"How was the service today, Len?" asked Mike, walking into the room.

"Good. You should come sometime," replied Leonard, helping himself to a beer in the fridge.

"Nah. Organized religion has never been my thing."

"I learned today that change must come from within if we are ever to grow spiritually."

"Great. I'll make sure to put that on my list of things to do next week. How are things out in the town?"

"No change," he replied, removing the cap and discarding it into the trashcan. "So, what are you and Amanda up to?"

"Ah, 'The Project.' Come on in and sit down. I'll explain."

The two walked into the living room to the blare of the television show Mike had been watching before Leonard came in. Mike hastily picked up the remote control on the coffee table and turned down the volume.

"It's the Guys from GI," he said motioning to the program.

"Sorry, Mike. I don't watch much TV. Who or what are they?"

"Ghost investigators—a team of relative laymen who investigate paranormal events."

"Haunted houses?"

"Precisely! Amanda turned me onto it."

"She has you watching reality television now? That's some accomplishment, Mike," replied Leonard, as if he had been sentenced to a summer vacation slideshow.

"It's the content that has me intrigued. Do you know what she's writing her book about?"

"Sure—the haunted houses of Miller's Ferry."

"Yeah, it's something she started a few years back, as a result of her own personal experience. Now that shows like this are gaining popularity and there are so many of them, she's decided to start it up again."

"How exciting," replied Leonard, acting impressed as he sat down on the sofa. "What's your role in all of this?"

"Oh, well she came over to ask about some of the stories that have circulated about my house."

"You have a ghost?"

"Not that I've ever seen, but I have to admit it was one of the reasons I chose to buy this house."

"So do you have a moaner, a chain rattler, or something that goes bump in the night?"

"The last owners reported that on a number of occasions, they saw a little boy in gray shorts and a cap. After digging through a lot of the old photographs at the Historical Society, they thought they might have identified him as member of a family who lived here during the great flood of 1909, a young victim of the treacherous rising waters."

"Come on, Mike! Don't tell me you believe in that supernatural crap."

"Why do you go to church every Sunday, Len?"

"I've always gone to that church."

"Yes, but why?"

"I don't know. To get right with God?"

"And do you know of this God? Have you ever seen Him or conversed with Him?"

"It's a matter of faith, I guess."

"Exactly. If one were to ask for proof of His existence, my counter as a philosopher would be to inquire for the proof that He does not exist."

"That's why I'll never argue with a philosopher."

"What I'm trying to get at, Len, is that as long as men have been alive to tell tales to one another, they have told of their experiences with ghosts. These fellows on the TV actually go to these houses without bias, seeking verification of some spectral anomaly through the use of modern technology."

"Do they ever find anything?"

"Sure, although most times it is beyond explanation."

"It sounds to me like they're looking for animals in the shapes of clouds."

"Say what you want, but this is one of the most popular shows on cable—for good reason, in my opinion."

"What's that guy doing there on the left?"

"He's making an audio recording while walking through the house. Oftentimes, they pick up things we cannot readily hear or can interpret. Later, they'll run it through computer analyzers to determine its origin."

"I guess you're a fan then?"

"I only just started watching yesterday, but yeah, I think I'm a fan."

"Where are they today?"

"Athens, Ohio. They claim it is the most haunted town in America."

"How can they claim that?"

"Through stories handed down and through investigations like these."

"This doesn't prove anything. Look at him skulking about in the dark." Leonard tipped his bottle back for a sip and then put the bottle onto the coffee table.

Mike reflexively slipped a coaster under it before it made its final landing.

"The most haunted town in America? Where do they get off saying that? Anyone could make themselves the most haunted town in America."

As the words left Leonard's lips, gears of thought slowly began to roll into motion. He replayed those words and the contents of their previous conversation over again, removing the pertinent parts for further processing. By the time he returned to his last sentence, Leonard's mind was in full production.

"Who's to say we're not the most haunted town in America?"

"No, Athens is the most haunted town. The GI specialists are there to prove it."

"They are no more going to prove that Athens is the most haunted town than I could disprove it. Isn't that what you said?"

"Well, sure, I guess."

"So who alive could disprove the fact that Miller's Ferry is the most haunted town? There's going to be a book written about our town. Do they have a book?"

"I don't know, Len. I guess."

"And these guys running around in the dark… who has certified them to be so-called Ghost Investigators? Is there some convening authority that deems them, above all others, to be competent in the field of investigating spectral anomalies?"

"Well, no. They just have their open minds and the tools of their trade."

"What if you had the tools of their trade, Mike? Could you be a GI?"

"Len, where are you going with this?"

"What if you and Amanda became your own version of the Guys from GI for this town? It could really bring her book together. How much could all that Flash Gordon stuff cost anyway?"

"Len, what are you up to?"

"I think I found my one good idea!"

Richard's Barber Shop opened every day except Sunday, always promptly at seven o'clock, although he generally didn't see customers come through his door until after nine. Many days he had no customers at all, but he never felt the least bit lonely, as his waiting chairs were usually filled with no less than five people at a time, there to gossip about the politics in the town, the state, the country, or just to find out what the high school scores were. This special collective of worriers, thinkers, statesmen, and debaters liked to consider themselves the conscience of the town, but in truth, they were just older men, mostly retired, with time to fill and gossip to pass.

Leonard sat in the barber chair with a brightly colored sheet draped about his body as Richard commenced with the preliminary scissor work. In the chairs were six men sipping on Richard's coffee, discussing the merits of the current president and his social habits.

"It seems to me he'd probably be a beer-drinking man," stated George Schuler, a retired autoworker. "Sure, he'll drink wine at the State dinners, but when it's just him alone in the White House kitchen, I'm bettin' it's a beer he's drinkin'."

"I'm with George on this one—definitely a beer man," added Ryan Crenshaw, retired ironworker.

"I don't know," responded Arthur Benze, semi-retired owner of Bennie's Beef and Ale Tavern out on the state route. "Seems to me, as leader of the most powerful nation in the world, he needs to perpetuate the image of Commander in Chief on and off the clock. He's drinking wine."

The remaining three men all nodded in quiet assent to all of the points made, holding back any opinion of their own on this delicate matter.

"I hear you, Artie, and on some levels, I agree. But I don't care what your job is. You are what you are, and I think at heart, the man's a beer drinker," countered George.

"I suppose so, but domestic or import?"

"With his foreign trade policy, definitely domestic."

"You know," interrupted Ryan, "most domestics are now owned by foreign companies."

The silent three all nodded their heads vigorously to this last statement.

"Now, given how he feels about foreign trade, how do you think he feels 'bout foreigners owning American beer?"

"That's a tough one," replied George. "On one hand, the beer is made in the U.S., employing U.S. workers. On the other hand, the money is leaving the country. I think he'd feel conflicted on this matter and only drink a beer that is made in the USA by a U.S.-owned brewery."

"Or maybe he just says 'screw it' and drinks California chardonnay," shot back Arthur.

"You think he drinks white wine? Why not red?" asked George.

Arthur rolled his eyes and picked up a section of the newspaper, thumbing through its pages to signify his participation in this conversation had reached its end.

Taking advantage of the conversational lull that was settling in, Leonard interjected, "Any of you fellas believe in ghosts?"

"Well, that all depends on what kind of ghosts you're talkin' 'bout, Mr. Mayor," replied George.

"The house kind. You know, disembodied spirits stuck between this world and the next."

"Hmm. Seems to me Jake at the garage was tellin' folks some time back that he had a Civil War soldier lurkin' around in his house."

"Did you believe him?"

"Never known Jake to lie... except when he comes home from fishin'." The rest broke out in a low laughter. "Why you askin'?"

"The professor next door to me is helping Amanda Bremner with a book she's been working on about the alleged haunted houses of Miller's Ferry, and Mike is going to be doing some ghost hunting in his house and mine. I'm fixin' to get my house in that book."

The six quietly conferred amongst themselves for a few minutes, until George Schuler spoke on all of their behalf. "You think he might be interested in doing our houses too?"

"Len, what have you done?" demanded Mike, storming through his friend's front door.

"Sit down, Mike. Can I get you a beer?"

"No thank you," he replied, taking up station on the couch across from Leonard.

"I take it you've had a few phone calls today."

"I stopped answering the phone after the twentieth call, but that didn't stop them from filling up my answering machine. What've you been tellin' people?"

"That you hunt ghosts."

"What possessed you to go around saying something like that?"

"Because you need this Mike, and I think I'm on to something that could really help this town."

"I don't need this! Have you forgotten I am retired?"

"You are no more retired than I am. What did you think you were going to start doing with your time, sitting around the house in your underwear, surfing for porn on the Internet all day? You've worked your whole life, and without hands that are busy and a mind to stay focused on a project, you'll be dead in five years. You know it and I know it."

"But where do you get off saying I can hunt ghosts?"

"Find me one person who says you can't. Those fellas on the TV show, what were they doing before they were the Guys from GI?"

"Electricians, I think."

"So what was their special training for this gig, huh?"

"None, I suppose. But—"

"But nothing. This interests the hell out of you, doesn't it?"

Mike tried to avoid Leonard's truth-exposing stare, with no success.

"I'll take your silence as 'yes.' How much would it cost for startup equipment?"

"About $8,000."

Len raised his eyebrow into an I-caught-you arc.

"Okay, okay. So I looked it up. I was just curious—and there are better things to surf the Internet for than porn, thank you."

"I'll front you the cash, Mike, and you'll have it paid back and making a profit within a month. I guarantee it."

"This is crazy, Len! I wouldn't even know how much to charge."

"So charge $500."

"Where'd you get that number?"

"It's the perfect number. Anything lower, you'll look like a fly-by-night, and anything more, people won't think you're worth it… $500 is perfect."

"What if they can't afford it?"

"They'll find a way—any way—when it comes to proving their houses are haunted."

"What if the houses aren't haunted?"

"Do the Ghost Investigators ever really prove a house isn't haunted?"

"Hmm, not really. If they don't find anything significant, they pretty much flip-flop around on it. 'Maybe it is, but we're just not seeing it' or 'That doesn't necessarily mean there is nothing.'"

"Sounds like a bunch of philosophy majors to me. So, you go into the houses and shoot some film footage, wave your gizmos around, record the sounds of creaking and groaning timbers, and declare an anomaly."

"How exactly does this help the town?"

"We are going to be the most haunted town in Ohio."

"Sounds like a confidence scam to me."

"Oh, come on, Mike. You may actually find something, and if you don't, you present what you did find as something open to interpretation. People will read tomes into whatever you say and believe what they want to believe."

"I can see you've really been thinking about this."

"I'm onto something here, Mike. I was thinking that after your investigation of a house, we can allow the owner to apply for a specialized permit, some kind of 'alternative zoning,' that will allow for paying tours of their haunted premises during special weekend events."

"You know, I'm starting to buy into this nonsensical scheme of yours. Haunted tours are big business in some cities."

"Do you really want another summer of car shows?"

"Oh please."

"I really believe we can start filling the streets with visitors, Mike, and every single one of them will at some point think about how great it would be to live here. Who wouldn't want to live in the most haunted town in Ohio? Folks in town will start making money and declare bragging rights over their homes. Hell, they might actually start feeling a little bit of pride in Miller's Ferry again. I think we finally found a pretty solid hook."

Mike sat back and chewed on this new idea for little while and then sighed. "I'll talk to Amanda and her husband, but I'm pretty sure the answer is going to be 'yes.'"

"Then we're in business. You want that beer now, buddy?"

CHAPTER FOUR

After making his initial rounds throughout the Ferry Landing, Leonard arrived at the chosen table, a changed man from the one just days prior.

Beatrice of the Historical Society was the first to greet him. "Good morning, Mr. Mayor. Won't you have a seat next to me?"

"Morning, Bea. Thank you," he replied, sitting down in the vacant chair next to hers. "So let me have it. What did you all think of the town hall meeting last night?"

"What a crock of shit!" replied Robert. "We're into the ghost-hunting racket now? Sounds like you're planning to turn this town into a three-ring circus, if you ask me."

"Oh come on now, Robert," interrupted his brother. "Unorthodox, maybe, but I think Len is onto something. Am I to understand," he continued directing his attention to the Mayor, "that someone is going to be writing a book about our town?"

"Sure thing, Ernie. Amanda Bremner is, with the help of Professor Pennington."

"Oh, Amanda. Nice girl. I know her father well," he declared unnecessarily. In a place as small as Miller's Ferry, everybody knew everyone.

"She's been working on it for a while, and with any luck, she'll be able to go to publication soon."

"Now what of this so-called 'alternative zoning,' Len? How does that work exactly?"

"It's basically a stripped-down version of our business zoning, allowing the recipient to use their property as a revenue-generating source, so long as they remain within the Act of Haunted Tourism."

"What qualifies the owner for this zoning?"

"Simply put, it has to be haunted."

"And how do you go about proving that?"

"Professor Pennington has been putting a lot of time and research into the creation of a new business called Spectral Investigations, or SI. He'll be using state-of-the-art equipment to verify the existence of any ghostly presence."

"Oh my," said Bea. "Will he really see ghosts?"

"Well, sort of. I'm really not sure how it all works, but with his equipment, he'll be conducting several tests to prepare his final report for each residence. At very best, there is verifiable evidence of a haunting, but for permit purposes, we will accept, at very least, any anomaly that defies explanation or interpretation."

"I see. It all sounds so very exciting."

"Well, Bea, it's going to make your Historical Society very busy. In addition to the report, the owner must provide as complete a history of their house as possible before applying for a permit. You know, I wanted to catch up with you at some point to discuss brass placards that could be affixed to the zoned houses. How does your schedule look today?"

"For you, Len, I'm wide open all day." She paused and turned a deep shade of red. "Oh dear! That didn't come out right at all. I meant, come on over whenever you want."

"Thank you, my dear. Perhaps some time after lunch."

"Now, what about this Haunted Tourism you mentioned, Len?" asked Tom of the Drescher Four.

"Glad you asked. What you folks will have to work out is developing special weekends to showcase Haunted Miller's Ferry. We still have plenty of time as we work out the zoning permits and get Amanda's book to print, but our primary focus will be Cincinnati. It wouldn't hurt to start networking with the public radio stations and perhaps work on some kind of tri-fold pamphlet or brochure we could leave at visitor centers on the interstate. You're really going to have to get creative on this one."

"Is it going to interfere with the Drive-In weekends with the car clubs?"

"Oh, for crying out loud!" snapped Robert. "The mayor still hasn't sold me on this whacky idea, but even I can see it has more promise than those damn Drive-ins."

Tom, whose pride and joy was his '67 Mustang, started to reply, but then thought the better of it when he met the piercing glares of the anti-Drive-In solidarity about the table.

"It's okay Tom. We can still work on the Drive-Ins, but our primary concern is going to have to be this ghost business."

"Well, what sort of weekend events did you have in mind?"

"At this point, I think any idea is on the table. I envisioned Haunted Tours of the town, with paid tours through the zoned houses. It could be a real event during the months surrounding Halloween. I'm thinking we should stage some kind of visitors' gathering point up at Memorial Park, by the gazebo."

"Ooo," interrupted Beatrice. "What about horse-drawn carriage rides!"

"That's a great idea, Bea," encouraged Leonard. "At this point, it's whatever we make of it. When we get ready to move on this, I'll see if I can't get the city paper out here to help out. At this point, there are no bad ideas."

"Except for those lousy Drive-Ins," groused Robert.

"Listen, folks, talk amongst yourselves, and I'll check back in with you all in a couple of days."

As he walked away from the table, he could hear the dull murmurs rise into an animated conversation behind him. In fact, all throughout the restaurant, Len picked up key words in table conversations about the innovative ideas he'd introduced at the town meeting the night before.

Out on the street, shops were opening for the day, and their owners smiled at him as he walked by. The cordial greetings of "Hello, Mr. Mayor" were welcomed after the past year of near ostracism.

Entering the village administration building, he ran into Lori Sykes, his assistant, walking out of the police division. She had been his right hand since he took over as mayor of Miller's Ferry. The truth was, Lori attended to virtually all of the administrative details associated with the office, leaving Leonard to be friendly and charismatic with the village. Although the buck stopped with Mayor Grey, it had to pass through Lori's hands first.

"Good morning, Mr. Mayor," she chirped.

"Hello, Lori. What do you have in your hands there, something for me to sign?"

"Monthly reports," she replied, handing him the small stack of papers.

"Is it that time already?"

"You know it. You want some coffee, Len?"

"Sure, but only one this morning. I already had some."

"Stopped in at the Ferry Landing, did you?"

"Just taking the town's pulse while boosting my own, Lori."

"And how is our patient today?"

"A little more alive than yesterday. It's still too early to tell, but the prognosis is starting to look good."

"The phone's been ringing off the hook, and there're a stack of messages on your desk."

"What has been the tenor of the callers?"

"Mostly good. A couple people want to have you impeached, but overall, everyone seems quite enthusiastic."

"Well, you can't please all of the people all of the time."

"Len, that was quite a bomb you dropped last night. You could have given me a heads up."

"I thought I'd surprise you. So, what did you think?"

"It's crazy, but it has put some excitement back into this sleepy little town, and that's good to see."

"Do you think it'll give them some hope?"

"Like you said, the prognosis is looking good."

Lori's outer office was orderly and pristine, as it always was. Plants had already been watered, pencils already sharpened, and the desk was arranged in neat piles organized by their level of importance. He opened the door to his own office and turned on the light.

Len smiled and walked over to his desk. Although he was no slob, the mayor's office was a different world as compared to that of his streamlined assistant. Hanging on the walls were framed front pages from his last place of employment, depicting news of significance that had occurred on his watch. On his bookshelves were volumes of ordinances and decrees that dictated how the village was to be managed, along with a clutter of trophies and awards from earlier days of coaching little league baseball. His desk was scattered with paperwork requiring his attention, placed in chronological heaps, some dating back several weeks. By nature, he was not very attentive to his paperwork and often required Lori's help in clearing his desk, in hopes of returning any semblance of order to his universe.

He sat down behind his muddled desk and put the monthly reports on top of a stack of papers he had started only two days before. Thumbing through the messages, he found most of them were indeed positive, if not enthusiastic. It had only been one day since the town hall announcement, and people were already clamoring at the thought of having their houses declared haunted. He returned the messages to their already teetering stack at the edge of his desk and sat back in his chair as Lori came in with his coffee.

"What's on the agenda for today?" he asked, accepting the hot mug.

"The city manager wants to meet with you at ten, but you're supposed to be up at the elementary school for Career Day at that time."

"See if you can push him back to one o'clock. I don't want to disappoint the kids."

"The Ladies Auxiliary of the First Evangelical Church of Christ want you to have tea with them at that time."

"I see. And after that?"

"Mike Watson of the Rotary Club, to talk to you about their Induction Dinner next week."

"And then?"

"That should be about four, and your schedule is clear after that."

"Great. I'll see him then."

Lori returned to her office, leaving the mayor to drink his coffee and contemplate his day. Before he could take a sip, his phone began to ring. The number on the display, permanently scarred into his memory, indicated the caller was none other than his nemesis, Pam Holcum.

"Good morning, Pam. What can I do to disappoint you today?"

"Morning, Len. I come with an olive branch."

"Really? What can I do for you?"

"This zoning permit you talked about… I want one."

"That's fine, Pam. You need to get in touch with Mike Pennington, who will evaluate your house for spectral anomalies."

"Can't you just give me one? You kind of owe me… you know, for the neglected street."

"There is a protocol to be followed here. I can't just hand the permits out like candy. Besides, my office doesn't issue the permits. They do that down the hall."

"Fine. I'll give the professor a call."

"He's a friend of mine. I'll see if he can't bump you up the list some."

"Thanks, Len. You think this idea will really work to help the town?"

"We're hoping so."

"If it does…"

Here it comes, thought Len.

"…will I finally get my street?"

"Your street will be at the top of the list for municipal repaving."

"Yeah, but when will you actually get around to doing it?"

"As I've mentioned before, you'll have to talk to the city manager about that. Oh, by the way, Pam, while I have you on the line, I've been reviewing the tax records, and it seems you're in arrears for your village taxes."

"You'll get your money when I get my street fixed."

"How can we fix your street if we don't get your money?"

"I'll tell you what, Len. I'll give you your taxes when you reimburse me for my medical expenses."

"Why would I do that?"

"Because they were for the ankle I sprained tripping into the pothole that is my street."

"Fair enough."

"Bye, Mr. Mayor."

Before he could respond, the call was terminated with an abrupt click from the other end. He shook off the call and returned to his coffee, when the phone rang again. "Mayor Grey," he answered

"Len, it's Mike," replied his friend and neighbor.

"Hey, Mike. How's it going?"

"Busy. You really started something here. I'm going to need a second phone line at this rate."

"People have been calling here all morning, too, asking about the permits. How are you coming with your investigations?"

"Technically, I haven't started yet. I've been playing around with all of the equipment for the past couple of days. Amanda and I are going to do my house today and tonight for our first dry run."

"Great. I can't wait to hear all about it."

"Hey, listen, I have to help Amanda run some cable now. I just wanted to say thanks. This has been a real experience thus far."

"Sure, Mike. Bye"

What had started out as a philosophical argument on the prima facie evidence of ghosts had suddenly become the hope and future of a dying village. It may have been too early to tell where it was going to end up, but sometimes motion, regardless of aim, is enough, so long as it is at least moving forward. As the rest of the world outside crumbled at the foundations, the village of Miller's Ferry was boldly looking to the future—all with the help of its own dearly departed.

CHAPTER FIVE

A delicate smog forever hung in the atmosphere of Itchy's Pool Hall—a combination of the dust he refused to clean and the cigarette smoke he refused to police. Although Ohio had passed a law forbidding the tobacco indulgence, Itchy turned a blind eye and allowed his patrons to partake of their self-destructive habit. This was also his policy concerning the habit some of his patrons had of sneaking in their own liquor. He had no license to serve the stuff, but he never begrudged a man a few snorts between games, especially if they were sharing their bottles with him—a small price to pay for his blind eye.

As Leonard walked in, the sunlight poured in from behind him, illuminating all of the particulates suspended in the air. The door sprung closed and rang a little bell, alerting all to his entrance. Four senior members of the local Masonic lodge were at a table playing Euchre, quietly talking amongst themselves, oblivious to Leonard's presence.

"Good morning, gentlemen," the Miller's Ferry mayor boomed as he approached their table.

"Morning, Len," replied Herb Schlemer, the new worshipful master and elected leader of the group.

"You got room for one more?"

"It's Euchre, Len. Only room for four," he replied with iciness in the tone of his voice. The group continued to play without even looking up at him.

"Oh sure, sure. Sorry."

"I guess you're dying to know what our opinion of your new plan is," he continued, dealing out the next hand.

"Well now that you've brought it up—"

"Don't like it," he replied, while the junior warden, the treasurer, and the steward responded with looks of grave disdain, appropriate to Herb's feelings on the matter. "Nope, not one bit."

"What is it you don't like?"

"Making a mockery of our town and a mockery of the Christian faith, for starters. And you, a church going man? Shame on you, Len."

"Sorry you feel that way, Herbert."

The worshipful master glared up at him at the mention of his proper name.

If there was one thing the good mayor had learned from his association with Pam Holcum, it was how to needle someone at the most basic level. "Personally, I'm trying to celebrate our town, our rich history. As for Christianity, I challenge you to show me where the belief in ghosts is an abomination against God. You know, Herbert, many Christians question what goes on in that mysterious lodge of yours. Any abominations we should all know about?"

When they said nothing and just glared at him over their cards, he knew he had their attention.

"Listen, fellas, I'm doing what I can to get some new blood and new money into our ailing little economy. So far, I seem to be the only one concerned about it. Jimmy, how do you propose to get enough money to start repaving our village streets? Hmm? No comment, I see. Herb, it is unlikely we will be able support the EMS service for much longer. Any ideas? Bill, we can't even keep spare parts for our street sweeper, let alone run the damn thing. What would you do?"

The four men returned their attention to the cards in front of them in an effort to avoid his rationalizations.

"These are the ugly questions no one wants to address, with the expectation that the village leaders will handle it. Well, we have. We're in the ghost business now, like it or not. My suggestion is that you find some way to embrace it or come up with a better idea. Come on now... tell me hunting around for spirits doesn't sound like fun."

"The only spirits you'll find in this place are the ones in my hip pocket," interjected Itchy, walking up to the group.

The four men laughed briefly and then returned to their card game.

"Morning, Mr. Mayor. Why don't you leave these fellas alone and come on back to the office. I want to show you a picture of the new snooker table I'm getting."

The two men walked into the parlor office. Itchy closed the door behind them.

"Actually I could give a shit what you think of my new table. I just wanted to get you out of there before an ugly scene got even uglier. Listen, don't pay the naysayers no never mind, Len. I think the idea is pretty ballsy."

"I never believed for one moment everyone would be onboard, but I never saw the church card coming."

"Ha! Baptists play by a whole different rule book. You know that! Have a seat. You want a little something for your coffee?" he asked, holding up a pint bottle of bourbon.

"Sure, but hold the coffee."

Itchy turned over one of the coffee cups next to the coffee maker and poured a generous helping for his friend. "Here, Len," he said, passing the mayor the cup. Retrieving the open pint bottle from the table, he raised it for a toast. "To a better, haunted future."

"Tell me what you really think, Itchy."

"Me? I'm not really crazy about it, but I can see where it could work. At this point, I'm willing to try anything." Itchy walked around behind his desk, sat down, and put his feet up into their familiar worn spot near the edge. "My biggest fear is that it'll start attracting all kinds of freaks from the city."

"Money is money, no matter who it comes from. What if they were, say, prosperous pool-playing freaks?"

"I see your point, Len. What does the rest of the town think about this one?"

"Generally, they seem to like it. There's been a lot of interest in the idea since the town hall meeting, so we're moving forward on it."

"Not everyone is onboard?"

"Nope, as was evidenced by my encounter out there."

"Yeah, well you're going to have to try a different approach than the one you used out there. You done pissed off Herbert and his toadies."

"He just rubbed me the wrong way."

"Hmm, I could see that, but you're going to have to turn hearts if you're going to make this one work. You know, you have a real shot at reliving your moment of glory in the all-state game back in high school. Remember?"

"Oh please, Itch. I had nothing to do with that."

"What are you talking about? You were the team manager."

"More like a glorified towel boy."

"Then let me refresh your memory. Fourth quarter, we were down by thirteen, against that juggernaut team out of Columbus. The crowd had lost hope, the coach had lost hope, and worst of all, our team had lost hope."

"Please, Itch, I—"

"Defense was coming off of the field, and you could see the look of defeat in the quarterback's eye as he reluctantly put his helmet on and hesitated before taking the field. So, what did you do? You threw a water bottle at him, grabbed his facemask and pulled him down to eye level to give him a good talkin' to. We may never know what words of glory you said that day, but our team came back to rally in the last three minutes of play, winning the game by just one point. You're a motivator, Len. It's your God-given gift—and even Baptists can't deny God-given gifts." Itchy let the words hang in the air for a little bit as he took a long, thoughtful draw on his bottle. "Now that it's just you and me, what exactly did you say to him?"

"I told him if he could pull it off, there'd be keg party at my house after the game. That's all."

"Ha ha! You kill me, old man, you know that? A keg party? Really?"

"Sorry, Itch. Some things are better left to remain the stuff of legends."

"Fair enough. How're you doing over there?"

"Could use a refill," replied Leonard, getting up from the couch and leaning over the desk. Itchy reached over from his sitting position and replenished the empty vessel. "I hear you, Itchy," he continued, sitting back down onto the sofa. "Hell, I think I've been this town's biggest cheerleader my whole life. I love this place, and I know we can do better."

"Well, it's the fourth quarter, my friend, and we're down by thirteen again. That town hall meeting was a good start, Len, but keeping hope alive may prove to be bit of a challenge."

"No doubt the biggest challenge of my career."

"Keep us going, Mr. Mayor. We're counting on you."

"Are you getting your place checked out by the professor?"

"What, for ghosts? Ha ha! Not likely. How about you?"

"Between you and me, I really don't buy into this stuff anymore than you do, but going through the cable channels, you can't deny there are a lot of people who do believe in it and will perhaps buy into our town once we declare it to be the most haunted place in Ohio. Yeah, I'll step up, maybe even get a brass placard for the front of my house. Hell, what kind of an example would I be if I didn't?"

"So this thing with Professor Mike, is it a con?"

"No more a con than what you see on TV. He's using the same equipment and procedures they're using to determine hauntings. I guess in the end, it is all a matter of how you interpret the data. The way I see it, it's like predicting the weather. You could give the same data to five different meteorologists, and they'll come up with five different forecasts."

"He staying busy?"

"Sure is. There aren't enough hours in the day for him anymore. We used to get together most every night for a couple of beers, but I hardly ever get to see my friend these days."

"He just retired, didn't he?"

"What does retirement really mean, Itchy? For me, it meant giving up what I had to do so I could pursue something I want to do. Mike's staying busy, that's all."

The two continued to sit and drink in silence for a while, as the conversation fell into a lull.

Itchy rubbed the stump of his shoulder and looked over at Leonard, who had been studying him. "What?"

"Just wondering, Itch, what do you think happens when... you know, when we die?"

"I try not to think about it too much. There are plenty of folks like good ol' Herbert out there who are hell bent on assuming me Hell bound. I can't say one way or the other where I'm heading—only that I won't be around here no more to hustle pool."

"I don't know what to believe. Mike says once our bodies die, they release the energy they once contained, and it is dispersed into the universe around us. Call it a soul or spirit or what you will, but he says there's nothing really spiritual about it—that it's all just a matter of physics."

"Well, he has a better mind than ours, but in the end, it's nothing more than an opinion just like everyone else's."

"It's all in what you have faith in, Itchy. Personally, I hope there's more than just this life. I do not want to believe one second we're here, and the next, we're nothing more than a memory, some dissipating vapor of energy. I really need for there to be more. I wouldn't mind hanging around for a while to see how things change."

"Yeah, and maybe haunt old Herbert," replied Itchy.

The two chuckled and toasted to the idea.

"I suppose I believe in God on some level, but I can't bring myself around to going to church," admitted Itchy. "I got too screwed up as a kid over religion, and I just can't do that to myself anymore."

"No need to confess to me, Itch. That's between you and your Maker. I wouldn't ever judge you either way because that's not my place."

"Plenty others do judge me. I guess I add a seedy element to Miller's Ferry."

"Who thinks that?"

"C'mon, Len. I hear the whispers and see the horrified faces when I go up into town. I'm the example every mother warns their children about. What do they think I am, dangerous?"

"Balance, Itchy, that's what you are. Light and dark, rich and poor—each defines the existence of the other. You provide social balance, my friend. I know nothing happens out here at night... uh, nothing happens out here at night, right?"

"Just drugs, gambling, prostitution, and the occasional virgin sacrifice."

"Right. Well anyway, pool halls have a reputation, a stigma, even if it is undeserved. The righteous and self-righteous can elevate themselves to ever higher levels of morality only because there is someone else contrary to their cause, someone they can rise above. Places like this become that forbidden fruit we have to exercise our free will over."

"How's that working out for you?"

"I gave up fighting the temptation a long time ago, you evil bastard."

"Ha ha ha! There'll always be a place for you in my Eden, Len. How about one more snort before you have to hit the road?"

"Like you have to ask."

CHAPTER SIX

The Lucky Chance Ranch occupied fifty acres of lush green pasture not two miles from town. It's eccentric and unknown owner wanted to establish a haven where horses could find boarding, training, veterinary therapy, or just be allowed to roam at will in large fields bordered by bright white fencing. The mysterious owner was a man of means, a lover of all things horse and cowboy, keeping the ranch as his one extravagance in an otherwise simple life.

The main house was for the ranch manager and his family. Just a stone's throw from the stables was the bunkhouse for the four hands that worked the farm. Two of the four had generally been transients, working with horses across the States, while they wended their way to different parts of the country.

Two of the workers were permanent. Angelo was the son of Italian itinerant fruit pickers. He had endured quite enough moving around during his childhood, and after a meteoric rise in his past career, he chose instead to leave it all behind and content himself to settling down and living out the rest of his life at this ranch.

The second was an odd fellow who lived his life as if he were the star of a cowboy feature movie, adopting the dress and mannerism of all of his favorite Western heroes. Most people in town referred to him simply as 'Belt Buckle Bob.'

Upon observing the huge gold and brass fastener with which he insisted on using to hold up his pants, there remained no mystery as to the origins of his nickname.

Upon the conclusion of his customary after-dinner nap, Bob swung his feet out of his bunk and slapped them onto the worn, unfinished plank floor of the bunkhouse. It was a Saturday night, and the transients had already fled to the city for a night of debauchery.

Angelo sat on the edge of his own bunk, looked over to him and smiled. "You heading into town tonight, Bob?" he asked.

"Yep."

"Gonna sing some karaoke up at the saloon?"

"Yep."

They were the same questions that had elicited the same responses every Saturday night for the past twelve years. The two knew everything that needed knowing about one another, which had been quite a challenge for Angelo, given Bob's propensity to reply in monosyllabic answers. They worked well together, had grown to be the best of friends, and at this point in their lives, had adopted their routines as a way of life. Angelo and Bob predictably played the roles of their script without change, not so much out of tradition, but more so out of a simple fraternal connection.

"You have any new lady friends up there?"

"Nope."

"Their loss. Maybe tonight, huh?"

"Yep."

Bob went through his routine of selecting the perfect rodeo shirt out of the three he had, the denim stepping-out pants he kept reserved for this weekly occasion, and his black, silver tipped leather boots buffed to a high sheen. Once dressed, he would ceremoniously fasten his belt around his waist with the signature belt buckle and then don a black Stetson cowboy hat on his way to the door. "Don't wait up, partner," he said on his way out into the cool evening.

He always walked into town. In fact, he walked everywhere. Whether it was because he wouldn't or couldn't drive was known only to Angelo. He was a familiar sight along the shoulder of the road leading into Miller's Ferry, where he ambled along with his thumbs tucked into his front belt loops. The cries from passing cars to "Get a horse!" were common, but he paid them no mind. When heavy snow left the roads devoid of cars, he would occasionally ride his horse into town, but every other time, he preferred to trek the journey on foot.

Bob's behavior was thought by most to be odd. He was one of those characters that stood out in sharp contrast against what was considered normal in a small town. The consensus was that he was 'not quite right in the head,' a fact that was hard to dispute when he did little in the way of explaining himself. He knew from the age of ten—the summer he had spent on his uncle's horse farm in Kentucky—that he was going to grow up to be a cowboy. He was born 100 years too late and a 1,000 miles too far east, but to his satisfaction, he lived the life he had always aspired to.

Bob was a very private man and carefully guarded two important secrets that no one in town (or even in his estranged family, for that matter) knew. The first was that his net worth was in excess of $193 million dollars, the result of a lottery ticket purchased thirteen years earlier. The second secret was that he was the mysterious owner of the Lucky Chance Ranch. He valued the anonymity he enjoyed in his own version of reality and used lawyers to create a paper front to mask his identity. Several managers had passed through the ranch over the years, never realizing that the bizarre man that mucked the stalls, mended the fences, tended to the horses, cooked over an open fire when there was a perfectly good stove not fifty feet away, or referred to everyone he met as 'partner,' was in fact their true employer. Bob lived to talk the talk and certainly walked the bowlegged booted walk of a true, honest-to-goodness cowboy.

He stood at the corner of the busiest thoroughfare in town. His stance was his own, somewhere between John Wayne and Gene Autry. He leaned way back onto his left leg, while the right was slightly bent off to the side, with the toe of his boot pointed out at a forty-five-degree angle, his thumbs still tucked into his front belt loops in cliché cowboy fashion. His hat rode low on his brow, just an inch above the squinted slits of eyes he used to observe the world around him. From his lips dangled a lit, hand-rolled cigarette from which he never inhaled; it was more for effect. He had never forgiven the tobacco industry for their contributions to the demise of The Duke, the great John Wayne, but he felt the smoldering cigarette was a necessary accessory to his ensemble. The light was red, but that was not why he waited. He would hold this pose until the sun had officially set, upon which time he would make his way on over to the saloon, known to everyone else as the Stumble Inn.

Leonard was making his way home on yet another day when his stubborn old truck had simply refused to start. He walked up to the corner and began to wait patiently alongside Bob for the light to change. "Evenin', Bob."

Bob slowly turned his head to face the mayor, but said nothing.

"Heading over to the saloon for a little karaoke, are you?"

"Yep."

"Country or Western tonight?"

"Yep."

Having exhausted all of his subjects for any further conversation, Leonard stood in uncomfortable silence, waiting for the light.

"Been hearing things," Bob continued.

"What sort of things?"

"Ghost things."

"I see. What do you think?"

"And they think I'm crazy," he replied, turning his head back to face the setting sun. "Hmm… might just work."

"Thank you, I guess."

The light brought opposing traffic to a halt, so Leonard took his cue to leave Bob's company.

"Well, I'll be hitting the trail now. See you around, Bob."

"Yep. Happy trails, partner."

CHAPTER SEVEN

As Mike Pennington and Amanda Bremner set up the last of their cameras, Leonard began feeling displaced by their investigation at his house. Video and thermal cameras, along with boom microphones, connected by miles of cable, had been set up in every room, including the basement and attic. They rushed about, laying out the tools of their trade, oblivious to his presence in what was now more their workplace than his domicile. In the past half-hour, the two had picked up their pace as the sun fell below the horizon; they wanted to get an early start and a finish to this investigation.

"So why do I have to leave my own house, Mike? I wanted to watch how this thing works."

"This *thing* is an objective investigation into any potential paranormal anomalies that may or may not exist within your house, Len. Your presence will only interfere and possibly even jeopardize the integrity of our findings."

Leonard resented the newfound snobbery his old friend had recently acquired through the business he was mostly responsible for starting. "Oh come on! This is me you're talking to."

"Exactly. I know how you really feel about all of this stuff, and I'll only resent you hanging around and poking fun at the work we're doing."

"Work?"

Mike laid a coil of cable down and focused on his belligerent friend. "Do you see what I mean? I have to tell you, when I first started this, I had my own doubts—like I was taking advantage of good people—but, Len, what we've been finding has opened up my mind to all kinds of possibilities. The things we have recorded and observed defy any real explanation. I guess what I'm trying to say is that I am now a believer. Now please, leave us to do our jobs for the next few hours. Why don't you go hang out at my place for a while?"

"Alright, fine. Do what you have to do. I think I'll go down to the bar. Belt Buckle Bob is singing tonight."

"Oh? No kidding! He does Hank Williams better than Hank Williams. Are you going to do your Bobby Darren?"

"I don't know, maybe. Let me know when you're all done."

As Leonard closed the door behind him, Mike continued with his task of cable running.

Amanda came down the stairs from where she had been positioning the last of their equipment. "All set up, Professor… and all the lights upstairs are turned off."

"Great, Amanda. Let me finish connecting this, and we'll get started. Go grab the EMF meter, the IR thermometer, and the EVP recorder. We'll start in the basement and work our way up on a passive sweep, then try interaction on the way back down."

"Sure thing, Professor."

After completing the final connections, Amanda and Mike turned off the last of the lights on the first floor and then, using their thermal imaging and night vision camcorders, they slowly descended into the depths of Leonard's house.

Like many of the older homes in town, Leonard had a dirt floor cellar. The ancient soil had not seen sunlight or fresh air in almost 200 years and had developed a sour, musty smell with the passage of time—an aroma the two paranormal investigators had now grown accustomed to in houses such as this. As they walked about the cluttered space, enhancing their visibility with a red filtered flashlight, they tried to assimilate to their environment and establish what was normal and what was not.

"Do you feel that, Professor? Cold spot."

"Take a reading."

"Twelve degrees from ambient."

"Stand back. I'll hit it with the thermal imaging."

"Anything?"

"Not really. Anything on the EMF?"

"Zero. Probably just seepage from the air conditioning unit over there. You ready to start heading up?"

"Yeah. We'll start in the dining room."

The two returned to the first floor and commenced their work in a similar fashion throughout the house, room by room, making sweeps with their instruments and recording the data. This was now their seventeenth house, and they had had become an effective, synergetic team. During these investigations, they interacted with one another to the point where they anticipated what the other was about to say. Through their deepening experience, they had learned what to focus on and what to ignore. In the beginning, they were in awe of everything that seemed even the slightest bit out of the ordinary, but as the practiced professionals they had become, they had much more confidence in their ability to discern. Now they focused on only that which was truly significant and went about their tasks as if it were all just part of another routine day at the office.

"How's the editing coming?" asked Amanda as they ascended the stairs into the attic.

"Almost complete. All in all, it's a quality book. I'm impressed."

"Thanks. I majored in communications, but I've always had a passion for writing. I guess English was my unofficial minor."

"Great. So far, I haven't really found any major errors—only a few typos. Once I'm finished, I'll pass it off to Len for a read, and then we'll work on the final proof. With any luck, he can get you into the publisher's office in about two weeks, maybe less."

"I can't believe this is happening so quickly. I can't thank you two enough for all your help... and for this job."

"EMF?"

"Zero."

"What does your husband think of all this?"

"Oh, he's been great, but I think it's starting to wear on him a bit. Thermal drop over here, six degrees."

"Negative on the cam. Yeah, I know what you mean. We've been at this nonstop. What do you say we take some time off and start back up again next Wednesday?"

"How does the schedule look?"

"Busy, but I don't want us to burn out."

"How's the backlog coming?" she asked.

"We're caught up to the last three, plus this one. I'll tell you what, let me do the processing so you can be a mom and wife again."

"Sure thing. Hey, another thermal drop."

"How much?"

"Big this time, twenty degrees off ambient."

"Whoa! Come here and check this out on the thermal imager. What does that look like to you?"

"I don't believe it! It's small, like a child."

"We've never seen anything like this before. Try interacting with it."

Amanda stepped away from Mike's side, and approached the area they were now observing. "Is there anyone there?" she called out softly. "We think we see you. Can you talk to us? Please try to make some sound."

Shhh… shoosh.. rrrr…mmm

"Oh my God! Did you hear that?"

"Yeah, and the EVP picked it up too."

"Can you tell us your name or how old you are?" Amanda's questions were met with what sounded like a low hum. "EMF has just taken a big spike… and holding. It's getting stronger as I approach it."

"This is unbelievable! Keep talking."

"When did you live here? Are you happy? Are you sad?"

The hum was now accompanied by a series of clicks and shuffles.

"The EMF is pegged. I can't get an accurate reading anymore, Professor."

"This is incredible. Wait a sec… shoot! I've lost it."

"It's back to zero. Temperature has returned to ambient as well."

"That was amazing. Let's go work the lower rooms and then let everything run on its own for another hour or so with us out of the house. We don't wanna spook the spook!"

After conducting interactive tests in the rest of the house, Mike and Amanda left the mayor's house and went next door, hoping to find him there.

After listening to as much bad karaoke as the average human ears could stand, Leonard had already called it a night and did indeed retire to his friend's house to wait out the investigation.

"Congratulations, Len!" Mike cried out excitedly, rushing in through the front door. "You're haunted."

"You mean I get my brass placard?"

"Is that all you care about? We just witnessed some amazing stuff."

"It was incredible!" added Amanda.

"Really? What did you guys find?"

"A few minor anomalies throughout the house and a big one in the attic."

"Wow. What was it?"

"I can't elaborate yet. I still have hours of audio and video to go through, but what we found in your house is probably the most impressive experience we've had yet."

"Don't think the irony is lost on me," replied Leonard with just a hint of cynicism.

"What do you mean?" asked Amanda.

"Oh, only that the most haunted house in town is owned by one of the biggest critics of your work."

"But all this was your idea."

"Don't let him bother you, dear," replied Mike, turning his attention to Amanda. "He isn't as, uh… enlightened as we are."

"I just don't believe it, that's all. You'll find I'm going to be a pretty hard sell, but I do still want the placard."

"Don't worry, Len," replied Mike. "Just based on what we have encountered, you'll have no problem getting your alternative zoning. I can't wait to start going through the rest of the data."

"Can I go home now?"

"Just give us another hour to let the equipment keep running. We've found that sometimes they pick things up once we've left."

"Great. I'll get another beer. Mike, Amanda?"

"Sure," they replied in unison, Mike smirking at the thought of being offered one of his own beers from his own fridge.

After Leonard had left the room, Amanda leaned in closer to Mike. "I just assumed he believed in our work."

"He believes in this for the same reason he goes to church—just in case there is a God. I love my friend, but in some things, the waters do not run all that deep, if you know what I mean."

"Do you believe in God, Professor?" she asked with the wide-eyed innocence of the truly faithful.

"Oh, heavens no! I'm an atheist."

"I see," she said, sitting back into her chair seeming none too impressed.

"But check back with me some other time in the future. These days, I find myself asking the bigger questions I never would have considered as an ideological young man."

Leonard returned carrying three beers and passed off one each to Amanda and Mike. "So what happens next?" he asked, returning to the couch.

"Well, first we go through all of the video and audio recordings for each room."

"That'll take a while, right?"

"It's not as bad you might think. You go into a zone, and before you know it, you're done."

"What do you see?"

"Most of the time nothing. Sometimes we see what looks like a shadow or even a small ball of light. We also go through the audio at the same time, and if there is anything outside the normal silence, we enhance it and study it."

"Sounds mind numbing."

"It can be a little boring sometimes, but then we come across one that really makes up for the all the rest—like yours. I'm looking forward to doing your house, Len. I think it will be quite interesting."

"Have you failed any houses yet?"

"I've found it really isn't a matter of pass or fail as much as what can be explained and what can't. But in your own terms, there have been three in which we found nothing."

"I suppose for appearances, there should be a few that don't pass."

"Len, I can't stress it enough. What we're doing is a completely legitimate, science-based investigation. Any more talk like that, and people may feel there is some kind of credibility issue. If you want this to help you sell the town, you can't short-sell our investigations."

"Sorry. Poor choice of words I guess."

"No, I'm glad you said it, because I've been thinking of taking these investigations to another level."

"Like what?" asked Amanda.

Mike looked back and forth between the two of them and then formed his words carefully to effect the proper impact.

"For me, it's not enough to just record data. I want to know more. I've been thinking of bringing in a parapsychologist and a medium."

Amanda blinked and sat upright in her chair. "I don't know about that, Professor. It sounds like something out of a Stephen King movie, and we don't want people to stop taking this seriously."

"Don't worry, dear. It won't be a part of our investigations."

"Then why exactly? The idea sounds a little 'dark arts' to me."

"It'll be more like follow-up work. There are only so many houses in this town we can investigate. It stands to reason that sooner or later, we'll work ourselves out of a job here, and I'm looking toward the next step. If anything, it will be more like a thesis study for my own benefit."

"Hmm. I've never really thought that far ahead. I suppose we could take this operation to other towns. I really enjoy what I'm doing, and there are so many tiny towns in Ohio."

"Yes, from a business standpoint, we could keep it going, but I don't know what kind of a place I'll be in by then."

"Other towns?" objected Leonard. "In case you've forgotten, other towns are our competition."

"Come on, Mr. Mayor. To us, this has become something much larger than brass placards," replied Amanda.

"Maybe so, but it is integral in placing this town on the map. I'm begging you to at least wait until Miller's Ferry is on its feet again."

"Relax, Len. That time is still a way off, and we would never do anything to derail your efforts," Mike replied in soothing tones. Turning to Amanda, he continued, "As for the business, I haven't committed to anything yet. Should the day come when I want to pursue something else, you can continue without me. I'd still keep a hand in it—not as your employer, but as perhaps your business partner."

"Wow. That came out of nowhere," she replied.

"The thought just occurred to me, and I think it's a good idea. Leonard over here got me started, and it didn't take me long me to pay off his loan. You can't deny we work well together, and when the time is right, I'd ask you to buy out half of what it cost to start this thing."

"But it's worth so much more now."

"In no small part because of you. You are as much of an asset to this company as anything else. So, what do you say?"

"Are you kidding? Yes, of course."

"I don't know, Mike, but weren't you supposed to do all that down on one knee?"

"Hush, Len, or her husband might get jealous. As it is, we both have to compete for her time."

"That's alright, Professor. John knows I love him," assured Amanda.

"And another thing, we're partners now, so there's no need for the formalities. You can call me 'Mike' if you'd like."

"I started out giving you the respect I thought you deserved, but now it's the only name I feel comfortable calling you. But I'll try... Mike."

"That wasn't so hard, now was it? As for you, Leonard, you are going to have to get the history report on the house complete before you can apply for your zoning."

"Oh yeah. That," he replied, looking down at the floor. "I suppose if I have to..."

"What does that mean?" asked Amanda.

"The mayor here is dragging his feet over having to go down to the Historical Society," answered Mike, "because he thinks Beatrice has the hots for him."

"There's no doubt about it, Mike," Leonard shot back. "When I met with her to discuss the brass placards, she became quite smothering, to the point of annoyance."

"You could do a lot worse, Len. She's a fine woman."

"I suppose so, but she could play a little hard to get. I mean, I'm one of the last great bachelors, and if she's to land me, she's going to have to use better bait and some new tactics."

"It's funny you should compare yourself to a fish. You know, it could mean..."

"Don't you go analyzing me, Mike," he interrupted.

"Never, Len, never. It was just an observation, my friend."

"Well, keep your observations to yourself. My life is not an open book for you to read aloud. And don't go wondering why I'm comparing myself to a book either."

"I was thinking maybe a newspaper, but what do I know?"

"Too much I'd say. Being my friend doesn't give you the right to pry into my life."

"Who's prying? Don't get so defensive over a little friendly advice."

"Advice is fine, but no more reading into what I say about myself."

"It's funny you should say 'reading.'"

Amanda giggled at the two bickering friends. "I'm sorry, Mr. Mayor. I couldn't help it. He is right, you know. She's a very good woman and a heck of a good cook."

"Thank you for the input, Amanda, but I'm not shopping for a relationship at this point in my life—or a chef."

"You don't have to marry Bea. Just try spending a little time with her. Who knows? You might just like her as well."

"What's with you two?" Leonard protested. "Since when did you get into the dating business?"

"Leonard, you have to have more in your life than just me," offered Mike.

"You're one to talk! Why aren't you out there getting into the game? Hell, you've been a bachelor your whole life, and you seem alright to me."

"'Tis a lonely existence, my friend. When I was young and good-looking, my life was filled with meaningless relationships with young co-eds who wanted to broaden their horizons. I am afraid the life I once had has left me ill equipped to cope with this stage of my life. I suppose if a woman fancied me the way Beatrice does you, I would be inclined to respond in kind. Let's face it, Len... at this stage in our lives bachelorhood sucks."

Leonard sat back in his chair, tiring of the confrontation, and took a sip from his sweaty beer bottle. He looked at his oldest friend and sighed. "So how good a cook is she, Amanda?"

CHAPTER EIGHT

Until eighteen years ago, the Miller's Ferry Historical Society had been the Miller's Ferry Savings and Loan. The final year of the bank's occupancy in the building had been a bad year for many saving and loan institutions in general, that one not-withstanding. The cause of its demise was not related to any kind of Ponzi scheme or bad real estate holdings; it had merely outlived its usefulness when a tri-state bank chain decided to set up shop in the new strip mall on the outskirts of town. Depositors were lured away by the promise of higher interest rates on their accounts, CDs, and IRAs, while enjoying lower interest rates on their home, car, and education loans. It was just another example of that which is outdated is replaced, so it seemed only fitting that it should be become a society that embraced that which is old, even historical. Along the walls inside, old photos of the once-proud Savings and Loan serving happy customers were displayed in conspicuous locations amidst the other village memorabilia, lest anyone forget the price of progress.

Leonard entered through the heavy bronze and glass door and was immediately greeted by Beatrice, who was sitting at her desk opposite the main entrance. "Leonard! How good to see you. I was wondering when you might be coming down here. Please, have a seat," she said, motioning to the old oak office chair next to hers behind the desk.

Leonard looked around, hoping anyone else might be there to distract her in any way, but unfortunately for him, they were quite alone. "Good morning, Bea. I suppose you know why I'm here."

"The same reason everyone has been coming here lately. I can't thank you enough for your idea. The interest in the old place has been overwhelming. It has really been a struggle as of late to keep the citizenry involved with the history of their own town, and now they're in and out of here every day for historical reports on their homes."

"Yes, an unexpected bonus, I'd say."

"That's putting it mildly. You know we're a non-profit organization and we have to survive on public donations. When times are bad, we feel the crunch every bit as badly as the hard-working souls who used to support us. Since the alternative zoning permit went into effect, we have already met our operating expenses for the year, and they still keep coming."

"That's splendid, Bea. Now I was wondering if—"

"There was a time when we used to swing a big axe in this town, Leonard. It used to be that you couldn't even paint your house unless we gave final approval. It was those pushy people in the mauve house on Cherry Street that changed all that. The house had been that color for as long as anyone could recollect. If they didn't like that color, they should not have bought the house. Living in the Historic District is a privilege, not a right. They made a cause out of changing the color, and in the end, guess who lost the teeth behind their bite?"

"You have to admit, Bea, it was a really ugly color."

"It was a Victorian color, one that had always been on that house. I don't care if it is ugly, Mayor. It was part of that house's history."

"I wouldn't know. Mine's brick."

"Yes, I know," she replied with a girlish smile, "and I have everything you want to know right here." She reached over to the far side of her desk for an overstuffed file and handed it to Leonard.

"Wow! I didn't know you guys had so much stuff here to research."

"Oh, you'd be surprised what we collect. Ordinarily, we just help people conduct their own research, but I just couldn't help myself when it came to you, Leonard. It took a while, but it's all here. Go ahead… look for yourself."

Leonard opened the file and sorted through the documents Bea had compiled. "You found everything—deeds, loan agreements, city citations, tax records. This is very impressive. Thank you, really."

"Oh, it was nothing for my favorite fella. You know, there have been nine families living in that house since its erection… uh, that is to say, when it was built in 1849," she corrected herself, blushing. "I made sure to include as many photos of the previous residents as I could find."

"Where did you get them?"

"Some were here, I got some from church records, and a few are from family descendants."

"I have to hand it you, Bea, you're very thorough."

"Anything for you, Leonard."

"Bea," he said, turning his chair around to face her, "I get the impression you like me."

Bea was taken aback by the sudden frankness of this statement. Searching for the right word to convey what she has always felt for him, she answered, "Well, duh."

"If you wanted my attention, why didn't you just come right out and say something?"

"In my time, Mr. Mayor, young ladies were not supposed to make the first move. For God's sake, Leonard, I've only been fawning over you since ten years to the day had passed after your last divorce. I thought it was an appropriate time to wait. Haven't you been getting my signals?"

"If I were blind and deaf, I still couldn't have missed your signals, Bea. I don't know what to tell you. I guess I felt I was no good at the relationship thing and figured maybe I should never be in one again."

"Relationship? Hell, I just want to have sex with you. I may be sixty-seven," she continued in a lower, conspiratorial tone, "but I'm very spry for my age... and very well versed in the Kama Sutra."

"Hmm. Did all the girls in your time study that?" he replied, leaning in closer to her.

"Time was running out, and I felt I should take some classes if I were to compete with anyone younger."

"I see," he said, sitting back in his chair. "Well, I'm glad we finally got this awkward little discussion out into the open."

"If you want, I could lock the front door, and we could do it right here on my desk—perhaps even in that pew over there from the old St. Matthew's church."

"Slow down, Bea! Slow down. I'm an old-fashioned kind of guy, and I need to be courted. What do you say we start with dinner first and see where it goes from there?"

"Okay, I can do that. Where would you like to go?"

"I was thinking perhaps you could make me dinner tonight, maybe at your place?"

A big smile spread across her face as she toyed with the pearls draped around her neck. "What would you like?"

"Why don't you surprise me?"

"Oh, I can do that too."

"I am sure you're full of surprises, Bea."

It had been a long time since Leonard had been in the company of a woman, and he had some serious doubts as to whether or not everything would work as it should, physically, that is. His doubts gnawed at him most of the afternoon, until he finally relented and made an immediate appointment to see his doctor.

Bess had been Doctor Berger's nurse since he opened his practice in Miller's Ferry a lifetime ago. Before the doctor saw anyone, they had to run the gamut with Bess, who took down everything before the doctor eventually walked into the examining room, and said "What seems to be the problem?" Fortunately for Leonard, he had chosen a particularly slow day at the doctor's office, for no one else was sitting about within the waiting room.

"Hi, Bess. I'd like to see the doctor," he said through the sliding glass partition.

"What's wrong with you, Mr. Mayor?' she demanded in an I'm-in-charge kind of way without even looking up from her paperwork.

"It's just something I want to talk to the doctor about."

"Whatever you need to tell the doctor, you can tell me. I'm a nurse. So, what is the problem?"

"It's something I wanted to discuss with him, uh, personally. Can I see him please?"

She looked up at him from the scheduling book she had been working on and put down her pencil. "Okay. Come on back."

Leonard entered through the door that separated the waiting room from the hall of examining rooms.

Bess intercepted him and led him down the hall to the scale, onto which he begrudgingly stepped. "Gained a couple of pounds, I see," she said critically, marking the new weight in his chart. "Examination Room Four." Bess snapped the file shut and hustled off down the hall to find the doctor.

The examining room was tiled, paneled, and sanitary like every other examining room in the world. With little else to do, Leonard tried busying himself with an outdated issue of Home and Garden and was immersed in an article about camping with toddlers when Doctor Berger breezed in, closing the door behind him.

"So you want some Viagra, huh?"

"What? No. I mean, uh… yes. How did you—"

"Bess. She can always tell when a guy is coming in for Viagra."

"God, how embarrassing."

"Don't be. She's a nurse. She understands more about your body than even you do, so relax. There is nothing you should feel embarrassed about. Now, when did you first show any signs of problems in that department?"

"I haven't—at least not yet. You see, it's been a while, and uh… well, I just want to make sure everything goes smoothly when I do… next, that is."

"You mean you need it for insurance, just in case?"

"Exactly."

"I get that a lot. Physically, Leonard, you're in pretty good shape for a man your age—"

"Watch it, Doc. I'm not that much older than you."

"Let me rephrase that. Of the two of us in this room, you are the one who is in the best shape. Is that better?"

"I can live with that."

"And I see no reason why you can't take it."

"Do many guys our age take this?"

"The easier question to answer would be, are there any guys our age not taking this? As our bodies get older, they stop working as efficiently as they used to. Many men our age take it just to keep the edge. And yes, I take it as well."

"Are there any dangerous side effects?"

Doctor Berger folded his arms and projected his best grave doctor expression. "In extreme cases—and I mean really rarely—the testacies have been known to explode."

In three seconds, Leonard experienced every emotion known to the male of his species, in addition to a few he made up on his own. He had to resist the urge to instinctively place a protective hand over his pants. "Blow up? You're messing with me, aren't you?"

"Yes, Leonard, I'm messing with you. Like I said, you're in good shape, and I wouldn't prescribe it if I felt it posed any health risks. Here," he said, producing two small boxes from his shirt pocket. "They're sample packs, five milligrams. Try it, and if you think it'll make the difference—and I know it will—you can use this prescription," he continued, handing Leonard a slip of paper, "but my suggestion is to just go ahead and get it filled. You'll end up using it sooner or later."

"You had this all figured out before you even came into the room to see me, didn't you?"

"Didn't I tell you Bess is very good at spotting the first-timers?"

Leonard lurked outside of the Village Prescription Center until the last of the customers had vacated, leaving the pharmacist alone for the somewhat embarrassing business that he had come to conduct.

"Good afternoon, Mr. Mayor. What can I do for you?"

Doug Zimmer had been the friendly pharmacist down at the corner apothecary for the last ten years. He was not a resident of the town by geography, but he was a mainstay within the community. Over the years, he had adopted a manner of speech that was, by its very nature, soothing. This was a valuable skill for a shopkeeper who usually dealt with people when they were feeling their worst.

Leonard stepped up to the counter and without breaking eye contact with Doug, slid the prescription across to him, face down.

Doug picked it up, quickly scanned the content, and looked up to give a slow, solemn nod. "First time, huh?"

Now it was Leonard's turn to give a slow, solemn nod.

"Don't worry. You have many friends."

"It isn't sitting very well with me, Doug."

"Why not? Is it the stigma?"

"Something like that."

"Forget about it. That was started by a younger generation who will be breaking the doors down to get at it when they are a little older."

"How about you?"

"What, this crap? I can still get it up. Can't you?"

Leonard's gaze hardened and began to burn a hole in Doug's forehead.

"I'm kidding, Len! Of course I've got my own little blue pills. I'm a pharmacist. You know, better living through chemicals? Like I said, you have many friends. You may be surprised to know who comes in to get these filled."

"Like who?"

"Oh, you know better than to ask that."

"Never mind." Leonard was in no mood for small talk, and with the conclusion of the limited conversation they were having, he shifted uncomfortably in his stance.

Doug said nothing, but continued to smile.

"Are you planning to fill that or what?"

The pharmacist responded by reaching under the counter and producing a small white prescription bag containing his medication, ready for the final sale. "The doc called it in. He was pretty confident you'd be paying me a visit."

"I feel like I'm the last to join some kind of secret club."

"Yet here you are. Want to see the secret handshake?"

"No thank you."

"That'll be seventy-eight."

"Dollars?"

"Sure."

"What about my insurance?"

"That's including your insurance."

"Jeez! It'd better be worth it."

"Some things in life are worth the price of admission, and this is one of them."

"Put it on my account."

"You sure you want to do that?"

"Why?"

"Pam Holcum's husband does my billing."

"So he sees what you prescribe me?"

"No, but there is only one thing in here that costs exactly seventy-eight dollars."

"How would he know... Ooohhh, right. Let's put this one on the credit card then."

Bea's choice for dinner had gone over amazingly well with Leonard, and he learned rather quickly that Amanda had been correct in the assessment of her talents in the kitchen. She had opted to serve a blackened Mahi Mahi, risotto with wild mushrooms and sundried tomatoes, along with summer squash, al dente.

Leonard worked at the thin film on his plate, all that was left, with a piece of her home-baked sourdough bread. "Bea, that was wonderful. Where did you learn to cook like that?"

"Oh, I took a few classes."

"You seem to do that quite often."

"What can I say? I'm a renaissance woman. Would you like some more?"

"No, please. I'm full."

"No room for desert? I made a cherry cobbler."

"Perhaps later."

"Alright then. Enough with the foreplay. Take me to my chambers."

"Bea, this is your house. I don't know where your chambers are."

"Oh, right! Up the stairs to the left."

"You don't expect me to carry you, do you?"

"You're not very good at this, are you? I see I have my work cut out for me. Just take me by my hand and lead me to my chambers."

"I need to go in the kitchen and get a glass of water real quick. Don't go anywhere."

Leonard fled from the table and dashed into the kitchen. After taking his 'medication,' he sauntered slowly back out into the dining room and held out his hand. "Come, my lover, and let me lead you to your chambers for a proper ravishing."

Afterwards, they lay breathless on their backs, staring up into the darkness.

"I thought you'd never finish, Len. You were unbelievable."

"Yeah I was, wasn't I?"

"You know what? That was all you, dear. That stuff you took in the kitchen takes anywhere up to an hour to kick in."

"What are you talking about?"

"Oh please! I'm not as naïve you think I am."

"Hmm," Leonard mused. "Well, you know what?"

"What?"

"It's starting to kick in."

"You're going to have to wait, Mr. Mayor. I may be spry, but I am still a senior citizen."

CHAPTER NINE

Over the following weeks, Leonard and Beatrice had become quite the item. Although they kept their relationship a closely guarded secret to avoid any unwarranted scrutiny, it had become a common, but unspoken fact by most everyone they both knew. In public, they maintained the same cordial relationship they had always enjoyed, but in Bea's chambers at night, their physical relationship had grown to the satisfaction of both. Furtive smiles and clandestine nods were their secret acknowledgements of their special time together.

There was nothing scandalous about the actions, but Miller's Ferry was a small town where gossip of any proportion came at a premium. In most cases, there needed only be an element of truth to a story before it became a wild and outrageous tale. In the absence of facts, the truth was marginalized in lieu of what worked to make the topic of conversation sound the juiciest. At this point in their lives, and their standing within the community, neither wanted to become the fodder of lewd and imaginative speculation.

The Group Whose Opinion Mattered Most was finishing a hearty breakfast at the Ferry Landing. Indulged in more of a meeting than an informal gathering, the group was all business on this particular morning. As per their usual seating arrangement, Leonard sat next to Bea in the warm glow of the morning sun that spilled through the lace-lined windows. He finished the last of his French toast as Bea secretly squeezed his knee under the table. The suddenness of the action caught him off guard, and his fork fell noisily from his hand onto his plate. He recovered from the surprise and addressed the Drescher Four. "Tom, where do we stand with the marketing?"

"We've developed and begun to distribute a brochure depicting Miller's Ferry as 'the premier haunted town of Ohio'," replied Tom. "Our budget was limited, so only two interstate rest stops have been hit so far. Once we get more resources, we can get better coverage at the stops north of here."

"Great. How about the radio stations?"

"That contact you turned me onto at the NPR station is really panning out. Amanda Bremner is scheduled for an interview on her book next week. After that, we'll get them to start plugging our first Haunted Weekend in September."

"Hmm. That doesn't give us a whole lot of time to prepare," interrupted Ernie Hoffler.

"We're further along than you might expect," replied Tom. "Bea has found a company in Cincinnati to conduct the carriage rides and has committed the Historical Society volunteers to conduct guided walking tours in town."

"Leonard, there's something I want know," asked Robert Hoffler.

"Yes, Bob?"

"Are you screwing Bea?"

"Oh my God!" said Bea, turning her head away from Leonard.

"Bob, what's wrong with you?" asked his brother Ernie.

"It's a valid question. Come on now. We're all thinking it—not just me."

"That has nothing to do with what we're talking about. Honestly, I don't understand you sometimes."

"That's okay, Ernie," responded Leonard. Bea snapped her head back around in his direction with a look of concern. "We may as well get it out in the open, Bea, since they already know. Bob, Bea and I have been seeing one another for some time now."

"Then why all the secrecy?" demanded Robert.

"I don't see how our relationship is any of your business. Now, can we move onto the business at hand?"

"What? I just wanted to know," he replied to the disapproving glares about the table.

"Bea, why don't you tell everyone about the tours," said Leonard, trying to steer the conversation back on course.

"Thank you, Len. Our primary staging area will be the park, at the gazebo. Volunteers will guide groups of ten around the town. Owners of the permitted homes will be dressed in period costumes and will conduct a guided tour of their own homes. Those wishing to take a guided tour of only the town can take a carriage ride, also conducted by one of our volunteers."

"What sort of charges can visitors expect?" asked Ernie.

"Three dollars per person, per house, and ten dollars per person for a carriage ride. If we get a good turnout this time, we might look into raising the cost per house to five dollars."

Everyone nodded their heads in approval.

Robert mumbled to himself as he ran figures through his head and looked up. "Ernie, that could be a lot of money. Is our house permitted?"

"No, Bob. You said you wanted nothing to do with this scheme."

"That could be a lot of money though," he repeated. "We have to get in on some of this action."

"You'll have to hook up with Professor Pennington for that," replied Leonard. "I'll tell you right now, though, that he still has a pretty long list to work through. It's doubtful he'll be able to work you in anytime soon."

"Hmm. I still think we should do this, Ernie. Make a phone call later and get that Pennington fellow over to our house. Offer him a kickback if you have to."

"Everyone, I have something to report," added Jerald Brauer. "My son told me seven people took their houses off the market since this ghost thing started."

"Really?" responded Leonard, surprised and pleased.

"I think it may be the start of a trend. Also, the houses in the Historic District that are still on the market have had many enquiries and at least two contracts."

"That is very good news, Jerald."

"There's something else," said a shy Jenny Kirchofer, raising her hand. "We're still broke, but of the people who are in arrears for their taxes, a good 30 percent have paid up, and 15 percent more have started payment plans."

"That is splendid, Jenny, just splendid. Did you hear that, everybody? People are starting to believe in our town again," said Leonard with a triumphant smile. "We might just do alright after all."

"And the money," added Robert.

"Yes, that too, Bob. Folks, you should all be proud of yourselves," he continued, putting his napkin on the table and rising from his chair. "In the face of adversity, we formulated a plan that may save this village. The future is still uncertain, but hope abounds. Times are tough all over, but people still need something for their leisure time. With local destinations becoming more attractive than those outside Ohio, I think we can provide something special here for our future visitors. We may not be a vacation resort," he added, putting his hands on the table and leaning in closer to the group, "but we're cheap, and we're close. We're going to put Haunted Miller's Ferry on the map. I can feel it in my gut people; we are finally on the right track."

"I gotta hand it you, Mr. Mayor, I think you got this old train wreck back on its tracks," said Itchy, passing a coffee cup partially filled with bourbon. "You really pulled a rabbit out of your ass with this one."

"Thanks, Itch, but it's still too early to celebrate. We haven't even had our first tour yet. I mean, it could be a bust."

"Don't be too sure of that, Len. You know what I had in here last night? A couple of Goth kids from the city."

"Goth kids?"

"Oh you know," Itchy continued, rounding his desk to take up his familiar station, "dressed all in black, creepy makeup, a lot of metal in their faces."

"No way! They must have attracted a few stares."

"No kidding, but I think that's the point. Anyway, they stayed for three hours and seemed to have a good time at the new snooker table."

"How is that working out for you?"

"snooker? Turns out my 'normal' customers don't understand it and haven't been playing it. Those kids were the first real action it's seen since I bought it."

"Hmm, Goth kids. You may have started something, Itchy."

"Not exactly what I was looking for, but their money spends just the same. Got me thinking of something else. I might put in a cappuccino machine, maybe even a music system."

"Aren't you the entrepreneur!" replied Leonard with a chuckle. "I just can't see you making espresso. You don't seem like the barista type, no offense."

"At three bucks a shot, I think I'd make more money at the end of the year than if I had a liquor license. It's just good business, Len. We may not be civilized enough for overpriced coffee, but those weird kids sure are."

"What kind of music you fixing to play?"

"Think I'll start out with one of them Internet jukeboxes."

"What is that?"

"Damn, you're old, Leonard. It looks like a regular jukebox, but instead of having fifty old records inside of it to be played over and over again, it accesses almost a quarter-million songs online. That way, any paying customer can listen to whatever they want."

"Wow! A quarter-million? I am old. I had no idea."

"They've become pretty popular in bars, and I can make some decent money off one. If this coffee thing takes off, I might even get the occasional band in here."

"I'm impressed, Itch. That's some pretty modern thinking. I didn't think you had it in you."

"What can I say, Mr. Mayor? I'm just a worldly kind of guy."

"You know, this kind of thing fits in with our vision of the future for this town. You know—kind of Bohemian."

"And less hillbilly, right?"

"One would hope. I've never seen a hillbilly drinking espresso."

"The world is changing," said Itchy, looking up to his ceiling, "and if we're to survive, we're gonna have to change too."

"I'll drink to that."

Leonard pulled up to the front of his house after a long and productive day of working the town. The old truck groaned and squealed to a stop under its shady tree. He made a mental note of getting it into Phil's shop sometime soon. The old truck was a familiar friend in Phil's garage, and the mechanics took special care in its maintenance. Their goal was to one day get it to the million mile mark.

As Leonard stepped from the truck, he heard a sound floating across his lawn—the sound of Mike's kitchen door closing. As Leonard entered through his own gate, he called out as Mike made his way to his Volvo around back.

"Oh, hi, Len."

"Haven't seen much of you these days, Mike. Guess you've been pretty busy, huh?"

Mike closed the distance between them as he approached the fence that divided their two properties. "What can I say? My job keeps me busy most nights. I feel like we haven't talked in forever. How're things working out with you and Bea?"

"Good, good. Turns out, she's a lot of fun."

"Is it serious?"

"Nah. Just fun."

"Oh, well. That's good too. You hear about Amanda's interview yet?"

"Sure did. Sounds exciting. How are book sales coming along?"

"For now, just local. After the interview, she's going to ask for a signing at one of the big book stores downtown. You never know… she might get lucky."

"I really hope she does. Everywhere I go, the news about this old town is getting better and better."

"It was all you, Len. I knew you had it in you."

"Thanks, but it was your inspiration. You have another house to do tonight?"

"Not tonight. I'm meeting with a woman."

"Oh really?"

"Not like that, Len. She's a parapsychologist and medium. She calls herself Madame Ovary."

"Madame Ovary? You're kidding! Sounds like a real whack job."

"The name has something to with giving life to the dead or something... I don't know. She has quite the reputation in the ghost world though. She is said to have helped the disembodied find their way out of this world and into the next for the past fifty years."

"Wow. I can only imagine what her resume must look like."

"I'll have to ask her about that over dinner. If I don't get back too late, will you still be up?"

"Doubtful. I'm bushed. See if you can pencil me in sometime soon though. I miss our get-togethers, and we've got plenty of catching up to do."

"Sure, Len. You take it easy."

As the two men went their different ways, dusk settled over the village. The days were starting to get a little shorter, the nights a little cooler. The birds were now returning to their trees, and the lights from every window up and down the street heralded the coming night. A few blocks away, Leonard heard Mrs. Zingle calling her children in from their play in the backyard. The football game at the high school had just started, indicated by the roar of faithful fans and punctuated by the brass and percussion of the marching band. This town is worth saving, Len told himself again, and it was a job to which he was very committed. He was not sure what kind of future was in store for Miller's Ferry, but does a drowning man question the source of the life ring that has been thrown to him? Nope, Len pondered. And we won't either.

Chapter ten

The week before Miller Ferry's Open Haunted House Weekend was a busy one for the little village, and now that their big night had finally arrived, Bea's Historical Society needed a revolving door to handle all of the excited homeowners coming in for costume fittings. Bea's collection of period clothes was a blend of garments taken from old attic chests, yard sales, and Salvation Army stores, each ensemble offering a unique representation of a different bygone era. For a modest donation to the Society, homeowners were costumed according to the point in time that their respective ghosts were once part of the living. It was another financial boon for the once-ailing organization, the idea of which was Bea's alone. Her inspiration kept her and her minions bustling about at a feverish pace, making her a person of respect and importance. She could not remember when she had ever been happier.

Life was equally hectic for Amanda and the professor, now partners in their paranormal business. Recently, two men in town had tried to assemble a business to compete with SI, but with Amanda's NPR interview and the release of her successful new book, she had taken on something of a celebrity status in the ghost-hunting realm, leaving would-be competitors languishing on the sidelines. Every day brought more clients into their hectic schedule, and for the first time, out-of-town requests began to slowly filter in. With the excessive backlog of work in Miller's Ferry, the two put the future clients onto a list not to be addressed until they had finished with their own town.

The professor was making his final connections to the equipment staged in the living room of an 1840 house while Amanda finished staging microphones in an upstairs bedroom.

"Are you almost finished?" called out the professor from behind a monitor.

"Almost," came the muffled response from a distant room above.

"I think it's dark enough now. Start turning out lights whenever you're ready."

A few minutes later, Amanda descended the staircase, turning off the upstairs hall lights once she made the landing. She looked over at the sofa, where a small Wire Fox Terrier bolted upright, trembling.

"Should we put her outside with the other dog, Mike?"

"I tried to, but whatever is outside seems to trouble her more than what's inside. I don't think she'll be a bother. She seems quite content to stay put."

The dog tried to understand what the motives of the two people in her house were, but she was too distracted by a spectral presence that only she could see.

"Look at her! She's terrified," said Amanda, sitting down next to the frightened canine. "What's her name?"

"I think that one is Janie, and the younger one out back is Dodger. He is apparently on patrol."

"Come here, sweetie." Amanda softly stroked the dog's back and gave her a reassuring pat on her side.

Janie tried to enjoy the attention Amanda was lavishing on her, but she couldn't break her gaze from the apparition that stood between her and the older man.

"And… that should do it. Are you ready, Amanda?'

"Sure thing. Let's get this done and get on home."

The pair grabbed their gear and headed down into the basement, turning off the last of the lights on their way. Stumbling around in the dark cellar, Amanda missed the box of plumbing supplies she saw on the night imager, but stumbled into a pile of paint cans and stubbed her toe. "Ouch!"

"Are you alright?" asked the professor, turning the red filtered light onto his partner.

"Yeah, I'm okay. You'd think they would have straightened up a little. Look at this place! It's a mess."

"Just watch your step. Hey, check this out," he replied, focusing his thermal imager on the far corner of the basement.

"What do you have, Mike?" Amanda asked, coming to his side and peering into the small video display. "Wow, that looks a person."

"I'll say. Try to make contact."

"Hello? We see you. Can you hear us? Can you talk to us?"

The collection of cool colors on the screen began to move, the blurred images of arms rising from its side.

"This is too much, Mike. Look at it. Can you make any sound at all?" she called out to the seemingly empty corner.

In response came a low mumbling sound.

"Did you catch that?" asked the professor.

"The EVP recorder registered, but I think the boom mike will have the clearer recording."

"What kind of temperature readings are you getting?"

"Wow! It's thirty-five degrees below ambient."

"No way! That's huge. Look! It's walking toward us."

The pair looked down at the screen in disbelief as the image on the screen grew in size. Amanda and the professor were suddenly enveloped in bone-chilling temperatures, which quickly passed.

"I think it's heading up the stairs, Mike. Come on... let's follow it."

They ascended the stairs as swiftly and as safely as they could, emerging into the darkened kitchen.

Mike scanned the room for any heat signature or other anomalies, finding only the pilot light on the gas stove. "Nothing. Let's check the rest of the house," said the professor, directing Amanda into the dining room.

"Mike, is it me, or do the houses seem to be getting more haunted with each job?"

"You know, I've been asking myself that same question. We've come a long way in how we observe and interpret, but nothing has changed in our equipment. You're right though. With every job, the evidence becomes more compelling."

"I think we're actually getting better data than that crew on TV."

"Wouldn't it be funny, Amanda, if Leonard was right, even if he doesn't believe it himself?"

"What do you mean?"

"What if Miller's Ferry is the most haunted town?"

"I think he'd brag about it, but he still wouldn't believe in it."

"Even with all the solid evidence I've shown him so far, he still can't wrap his mind around the idea of ghosts. All he wanted was his little brass plaque."

"It's a shame, and he has such a lovely haunted house. If you're going to have ghost, a little girl is the best."

"She was a playful thing, wasn't she?"

"Sure, but not until after we left the house. She's the only one to move the cameras."

"Oh, I know... and the pull-cord swinging on the shade. Remember that?"

"What year did she die?"

"In 1927, of pneumonia," replied the professor, maneuvering around the dining room table

"That's right. Poor thing is still hanging around, and with a host who refuses to believe she exists."

"I love my friend, but he is shallow of mind and short in vision. I've heard that man complain constantly about losing his truck keys. I'll bet you that little imp is hiding them from him."

"It'd serve him right for ignoring her! Nothing in here, Mike. How about you?"

"Only the dog. C'mon, let's go upstairs."

"What if the town is becoming more haunted as a result of our work?" asked Amanda as she climbed up the dark staircase behind her partner.

"You mean like a self-fulfilling prophecy?"

"What if they have always been here but gone unnoticed? Do you think there is some kind of other-worldy intelligence trying to reach out to us?"

"That's a big leap, even for me, but I am coming around. In the past, I've always believed these anomalies were just residual energy, like echoes from a long-silenced voice. After what we've encountered since starting this venture, I'm not sure what to believe anymore. Take a reading at the doorway over there."

"Nothing. I have to believe it is more than just energy," said Amanda, looking up from her instruments.

"So do I. That's why I'll be working with Madame Ovary soon. If I am to remain objective in my findings, I should be open to all possibilities."

"What is she like?"

"Well… interesting, if not a bit flamboyant. She has done some amazing things, and I think I'm ready to see her in action. If she is what she claims, perhaps we can bring her along for an occasional consult. Let's start in that room down the hall."

"What does she do?"

"She claims she can connect with displaced spirits and deliver them from this world into the next. Amanda, go over there next to the bed."

Amanda deftly navigated the darkened bedroom and stood at the head of the bed, next to the night table. While observing the meters in her hand, she felt a chill creep upon her, a tingling sensation rippling down her spine.

"Amanda, are you registering?"

"Mike, I've never seen the equipment do this before. Readings are all over the scales."

"I am seeing the perfectly formed image of a man standing right next you."

"I just felt something on my shoulder."

"That would be his hand. Say something to him."

"Um… we know you're here. Can you say something to us?"

A sound, subtle at first, as if it were a low groan detected from afar, built in intensity. It slowly developed into unintelligible utterances, followed by a distinctly pronounced word.

"Please! He said 'please', Mike."

"I know, I know. I heard it too. Wait, I'm losing him."

"I can feel him leaving. No, stay. Please stay and tell us what you want."

"My God, Amanda, that was amazing. I think we can catalog that as our first confirmed interaction."

"Do you still think they're just echoes?"

"I think I'm ready to make that leap over to your side."

"Bea, I think this dress is just too long. I'm afraid I'll ruin it if I wear it out of here."

"Nonsense, Pamela. Come here and let me help you out."

Bea guided the person she had been attending to the trunk full of hats to complete his costume and beckoned Pamela Holcum to come over to her desk. The Historical Society had been the center of activity all evening, as placarded homeowners bustled about in their costumes prior to their opening performances. Pamela gathered up the cascading material from her dress and shuffled across the room in her stocking feet.

Bea rummaged through the drawers in her desk until she found the elusive box of safety pins for which she had been searching. "Now stand still, and I can give you a temporary hem. If this is going to be your permanent costume, I recommend you take it to Ethyl tomorrow to have her alter it for you."

"I do like it, and it should work nicely for my ghost."

"You're the murdered housewife, right?"

"That's right. How did you remember that amongst all the other people you've helped?"

"That's the only murder this town has ever seen, as far as I know."

"No kidding? Guess that makes my ghost pretty special."

"Yes, dear, I suppose it does. There, that should do it. Try walking around some and see how it swooshes."

"It's perfect, Bea! Thank you so much."

"A little something in the cookie jar over there would go a long way in helping out the Society."

"Maybe even a big something," Pamela gloated. "Thanks again."

"Alright. Who's next?" Bea called out to the morass of spectral impersonators. "You, the Doctor Brown ghost, not the bowler. Go with the straw hat that is more appropriate to his period. Jenny, darling, you're never going to fit into that dress. Besides, your ghost was an immigrant housekeeper, and that look is much too formal."

The Historical Society had not seen so many people since... well, never. To its curator, the citizenry of Miller's Ferry awarded the nickname 'Queen Bea,' a title that suited her well, as she organized and costumed everyone in her busy hive. Her long-neglected Society had grown back into an institution of importance in her little town, and having authority was something she had desperately missed and welcomed back wholeheartedly.

"Kids, put those down. They are walking sticks, not swords. Jenny, please keep an eye on your children."

Leonard crept up behind Bea and startled her with a kiss on her turned cheek. "Hey, sweetheart. Looks like you're pretty busy."

"Oh, Leonard, you have no idea. It's been like this for the past five hours."

"Well, they better start picking up the pace. The first group is being assembled up at the park right now."

"Did you hear that, everybody?" Bea shouted above the din. "The first group is being organized. Let's move it, folks!"

The hurried pace quickly accelerated into a frenzy as those who had waited until the last minute buttoned and laced up their costumes.

"Honestly, Leonard, I hope it isn't going to be this bad every time."

"Yeah, but you have a handle on it. You've been doing a terrific job here."

"Thank you, dear. I took a quick look in the cookie jar a little while ago, and there must be over a $1,000 in there."

"Incredible, Bea. I really think we're going to pull this off."

"How many people are up the park?"

"Maybe fifty so far, but there are cars parked all over town. It's looking like a pretty good turnout so far, and the night is still young."

"Your nemesis Pamela was here earlier."

"Yes, I passed her on the street. You know, she was actually quite civil to me and didn't mention her road once. I feel like this is starting to bring out the best in everyone, even our detractors."

"You did it, Leonard. If nothing else, you made us all proud of our village."

"Aw shucks. Now you've gone and done it. I'm getting all misty over here."

Bea gave him a playful punch on his arm and rewarded him with her biggest smile. "Oh, hey, put that down!" she called out to a man from 1890. "It's part of the display. I'm sorry, Len, but I really have to get back to work."

"That's alright. I'll let you go. Good luck."

After exiting the Historical Society, Leonard paused to observe what was happening out on the street. All along the sidewalks, people were meandering about, most of them holding the new brochures the Drescher Four had recently published. A couple hustled past him, trying to catch up with a group that was raptly listening to the words of their tour guide, who enthusiastically read aloud from her tour script.

He walked, hands in pockets, the short distance up to the park, taking delight in all he was seeing. There were people everywhere. The locals were dressed in their costumes, while those from out of town eagerly stepped up to pay for a guided tour of what was advertised to be 'the most haunted town in Ohio.' They came by minivan, SUV, and sedan from counties all over, hoping to be a part of the spectacle. The horse-drawn carriage clip-clopped its way past him, loaded with excited passengers hoping to see a real ghost. As charged as the atmosphere was that night, no ghost need be seen to satisfy their curiosity; it was enough just to be a part of something this magical.

After being let in from his nightly backyard patrol, Dodger ran into the living room carrying a well-chewed tennis ball in his mouth. Five years younger than his sister Janie, Dodger was a boundless source of energy and entertainment to all. Nothing ever seemed to get him down, or slow him down, for that matter. When he wasn't sleeping, he ran everywhere, and when he played, he played with earnest intent.

He hopped up onto the sofa and dropped the ball next to his sister.

"You want to play with the ball?"

"No."

"How 'bout we play with the ball then?"

"I said no."

"Want to play 'King of the Couch'?"

"I don't want to play."

"You see him again, don't you?"

"He's right there, just staring at me."

"How come I don't see him?"

"I don't know."

"Think it has something to do with that pill they give you each morning?"

"What pill?"

"The one they hide in the food."

"You're kidding! They're medicating me?"

"Uh huh. Haven't you wondered why they give you some food from their finger before feeding you, and they don't do the same for me? I've watched them. They hide a pill in the food first."

"I wonder what kind of pill it is."

"I don't know, but they say it's because you're crazy."

"They'd be crazy, too, if they saw what I see every day."

"Weird. Hey, you want me to lick your ear?"

"Sure. I think I'd like that. Can I lick yours next?"

"Sure."

CHAPTER ELEVEN

The Sunday following Miller Ferry's Open Haunted House event was one of recovery. In all, the final estimate was over 2,000 people from out of town. Homeowners slept in from a night of tours that went on until almost two in the morning for visitors who could not get enough. As a result, pastors, reverends, and priests faced thinned congregations during their morning services and hoped this would not be an indication of what they were to face on future Sundays.

On Monday morning, the bank tellers were kept busy with long queues of customers waiting to make their deposits from the event. By the end of the day, the most successful homeowner turned out to be Pamela Holcum, whose murdered housewife ghost earned $3,298.

Success can be measured any number of ways. When one reflects on the past, it is common to dwell on the milestones in life and take the time to savor all of those individual achievements. Sometimes the focus is on the end, especially where it does justify the means. An accumulation of wealth is certainly worthy of the measure, but notoriety would have to be at the top of the list. Before the Miller's Ferry Haunted Weekend, there was little to measure in the invisible town's history. In the mere passage of two days, however, the town had morphed into something beyond all expectations. Things were changing for the little village, to the satisfaction of all.

When Leonard entered the Ferry Crossing, diners stopped all of their activities and fell silent, as if royalty had stepped into their humble presence. He looked about the room for some indication as to what the sudden attention paid to him was all about, when from the back of the restaurant came a slow and deliberate clap. The rest of the restaurant joined in, and the diners rose to their feet to applaud with great enthusiasm. For Mayor Leonard Grey, it was his first standing ovation, perhaps the greatest moment of his career.

He walked through the dining room like Caesar entering Rome, to the joyful cries of "Good job, Mayor!" 'Attaboy, Len!" and "Way to go, Grey!" People enveloped him, slapping his back and seizing his hand for shake after shake. When he walked into the adjoining dining room, the reception continued in grand fashion, with near deafening applause and cheers. He squirmed his way through the crowd and found his seat next Bea. She stopped her clapping and held him in a tight embrace, followed by a passionate kiss to the answer of whistles and laughter.

Leonard sat down in his usual seat next to Bea, signifying the end to the reception. All around the table, The Group Whose Opinion Mattered Most beamed with pride to be sitting with the man of the hour.

Nobody said anything for a long, awkward moment, until Robert Hoffler spoke first. "Nice job, you old son of a bitch."

Leonard chuckled and thanked him for the kind words.

"We can't thank you enough, Len," offered Tom Drescher of the Drescher Four. "If this is only a taste of what is to come, we have little to worry about. The initial estimates for this weekend are fantastic. We're guessing over $50,000 has been injected into our local economy, and those are only the conservative estimates."

"Our ghost made $1,200," offered Robert with pride.

"He's the tobacco merchant," continued his brother Ernest by way of boastful explanation. "We haven't seen him yet, but a couple of our visitors thought they might have caught a glimpse of something."

"So when can we raise admission fees?" asked Robert.

"That's up to the village," replied Leonard, "but my suggestion would be that we wait until we become a little more established before we do anything like that."

"Quite right, Leonard," jumped in Jerald Bauer, "and I think there should be some kind of monitoring to make sure we all honor the established admission fee."

"Do you really think that will be a problem?"

"You didn't see the business Pamela Holcum's house got, did you, Leonard?"

"No, why?"

"Her ghost is a murdered housewife," said Ernie, "and she definitely got the lion's share of visitors. Even after we went to bed, she was still taking tours through her house. Now, our ghost may not be exciting as hers, so she may feel that hers is worth more than ours to see or not see... well you know, experience. Anyway, I think you see what I am driving at. We shouldn't have to drop our rates to make sure we can compete, and she definitely shouldn't be allowed to raise hers first. All admission prices should remain the same."

"I think you're right, Ernie. We're still developing the market, so there's no need to mess with a recipe that works. We'll make sure to let all the zoned homeowners know the admission fees are not to be changed. Tom," he continued, turning to the Drescher Four, "I'm thinking we need to start a website."

"Splendid idea, Len. My daughter Lucy is up on that. I'll see what she can do."

"Oh, Len," interrupted Jerald, competing for the mayor's attention, "I took the opportunity to plug my son's business when I started hearing folks talking about real estate. I handed out almost forty business cards for him. He told me yesterday he's already received seven calls for appointments this week, and on a Sunday. Can you believe it?"

"That is great news, Jerald, great news. We're doing it, everyone!" Leonard continued as he rose to his feet, addressing the whole room. "Miller's Ferry is home, our home. I love this town and everyone in it. Until recently, there wasn't much hope left. Hell, I think most everyone gave up hope of things ever turning around for us, but here we are. And this is just the beginning, friends. We aren't out of the woods quite yet, but we're beginning to see the light. We still have the rest of autumn to get through, and maybe three or four weeks into the winter. It'll take a lot more work, but my guess is that by this time next year, the whole state of Ohio will find that Miller's Ferry really is back on the map," he finished in a triumphant cry.

The entire room broke out in another round of spontaneous cheering and applause.

If he had been running for president, he knew everyone in that room would cast their ballot for him. The mayor's office had been a lonely station these past years. Now, in the glow of his town's adoration, he felt it was all worth it. The measure of a mayor's success is best measured alongside his failings. Leonard had once been a popular mayor before this day, but that was the furthest extent to which his office ever went. Popularity alone was not enough to sustain his reputation, and the emptiness of mere existence had never been more apparent than it was when the town stood at the brink of the abyss. Suddenly, being the guy everybody liked paled next to being the leader who saved his village.

After a hearty breakfast, Leonard made his way down to Itchy's . Inside Miller's Ferry new Billiard Parlor, the one-armed man was pushing a broom across the bare planked floor, not as much a clean sweep as it was an effort to redistribute the dust and debris it gathered along its path.

"'Morning, Itch!" Leonard called out across the room.

"Well, if it isn't the conquering hero. I'd applaud, but I don't think you'd hear it. How 'bout I just shake yer hand instead?"

"Thanks, Itch. Why don't you take a break and make us a couple of your special coffees."

The two men disappeared into Itchy's office and took up their familiar places, bourbon cups in hand.

"So how'd you do this weekend, Itch?"

Itchy sat way back in his chair and looked at Leonard across the tops of his boots and smiled. "Unbelievable. I ain't never made that much money in one night. Man, I did better than my best week ever. I gotta hand it to you, Len, you did it. Won't be no time at all 'til we're back, rollin' on down the tracks again."

"What kind of customers did you have?"

"Had a lot them Goth kids back again, along with a bunch of yuppie outta-towners. Come to think of it, I don't remember seeing any of my regulars. They all had a pretty swell time, Len. I couldn't keep up with the coffee orders, probably because I have no talent in making espresso. One of them Goth kids stepped up and did real good at it. He did so good, I reckon I can work him every weekend now. Turns out, they ain't such a bad lot."

"Did you get a band in here?"

"Wasn't even looking for one, but this long-haired guy wandered on in and asked if he could play for tips. Did a fine job, and the folks sure liked him."

"My, my, aren't you something else? It would seem everyone did well Saturday night."

"Do tell. What of the folks uptown?"

"I won't know until the end of the day, but I'm guessing between the zoned homeowners and businesses, we may be looking at around $100,000. The Historical Society alone made a deposit of $7,500 this morning."

"I'm stunned."

"And that's not all, Itch. I drove around the Historic District this morning, and three more 'For Sale' signs were taken down. You know Bernie Weitze?"

"Sure, sure. Nice fella, as I recall."

"He's turning his house into a bed and breakfast."

"Don't that beat all? So Miller's Ferry has become a destination. I must say, you really are a hero."

"Not me. It was the town that pulled together."

"What a hook, ghosts. If you were to try and explain this hairbrained scheme of yours to me ten years ago, I'd have probably laughed in your face. Never saw this one coming. How you doing over there?" Itchy asked as he replenished his own empty cup.

"I'm good. The professor has been really busy. He's making a killing at this."

"Not bad for a retired teacher."

"Not bad at all. He's already made more money than he did all last year at the university. Amanda is his partner now. You know she sold three cases of her books this weekend?"

"No kidding! And it couldn't have come at better time. There're rumors of layoffs at her husband's company. He's a nice guy, kind of quiet, comes in here sometimes to shoot some pool on his way home."

"How's he taking all her success?"

"Hard to figure. He's a good man who wants to be a good provider. Oh, he's tickled pink about Amanda, but some men take it kind of hard when they think they can't be there for their families."

"They won't have to worry about money for some time."

"It ain't the money, Leonard. It's a matter of a man's fallen pride."

"I wish I could fix that."

"Well, don't let that take away from your good works here, Len. There are plenty of folks struggling right now, and they're making do. Hell, we could be a lot worse off, you know. At least now we have some direction again."

"Where're 'ol Herbert and his stooges this morning?"

"Ain't seen them in a while. It's hard to sit so high and mighty when everything you're against is working out so well. You put him in his place pretty good that last time you saw him, and I think he was humbled. Who knows? Maybe he's trying to come up with a better idea, like you suggested."

"And I welcome the effort if he is. This ghost thing is working out well for now, but I really don't see it as a permanent fix."

"What would be a permanent fix?"

"Commerce, Itch, plain and simple. A new industry or company that could keep these people working and paying their bills would go a long way. We need an entity that can turn a profit and throw tax revenue back into this community."

"That's a pretty tall order, especially in this economy."

"Well, I think for now, we've been given a little elbow room to work that out. With our ghosts, I'm hoping we can get some money flowing through our own economy, along with the hope that folks outside of here will take an interest in our little bedroom community and want to settle down. My hope is that one might bring the other. I know of thirty acres not five miles from here that are ready to be developed into a business or industrial park. All we need is another good hook."

"You really have been thinking ahead. You've done a pretty good job in dangling this one, so I see no reason why you can't pull that scheme off as well. You know, I don't think people give you near enough credit for what you do."

"Have I told how much I love this town, Itch?"

"I'll drink to that."

Mike Pennington lay in his bed listening to the phone ring downstairs. He had long since disabled the ringer on his bedroom phone, but the one downstairs was sufficient in rousing him from his slumbers. It was eight-thirty, and he had looked forward to sleeping in and catching up on his some well-deserved rest, but once again, his popular service prevented this from happening. He and Amanda had been working tirelessly, and he was finding that getting out of bed in the morning was becoming an ever-increasing challenge.

He sat up and swung his feet over the side of his bed and slid them into his navy blue slippers. He refastened a button on his plaid pajamas that had worked its way loose through the night and headed down to the kitchen for some coffee and breakfast. Upon making the landing on the first floor, he was startled by a rapping on his window and the face of a strange woman peering inside. He strode over to the front door and threw it open to address the stranger standing in his boxwoods. "Who are you? What do you want?" he demanded sternly.

"Oh, Mr. Pennington, thank you. I tried calling, but you wouldn't pick up."

"This is my home, damn it. If I don't pick up my phone, it's because I'm not available."

"Well, I'm glad I can talk to you now. I live on Arch, in the big Victorian at the end. I was wondering if I could get on your schedule, preferably soon."

"This is unbelievable! Leave a message like everyone else, and I'll get back to you when I can. Now, can you please get out of here?"

Mike slammed the door shut before the offensive woman could reply and stormed into the kitchen. On his way past the answering machine, he took note of the blinking number thirty-seven and shrugged it off. It was a full-time job just keeping up with messages, let alone the actual work they were bound to yield. He marveled at how quickly he had gone from the quiet life of a retired philosophy professor to that of a rock star.

As the coffee dripped, he picked up the kitchen phone and dialed his partner Amanda.

"Hello?"

"Good morning, dear. It's Mike."

"Oh, hi. I thought you were going to sleep in late today?"

"So did I. The phone's been ringing off the hook, the answering machine is overflowing, and I haven't even looked at my email yet."

"Oh, Mike, I'm sorry."

"How did it get like this? I mean, we don't even advertise."

"Word of mouth in a small town is the best advertisement you can get. It's been pretty crazy over here too. Not only am I getting the same calls you get, but I'm dealing with the book as well. It's starting to take off, and they want me to do a tri-state book tour."

"When were you planning on sharing that bit of information?"

"I'm sorry, Mike. My publisher talked to me about it last week, but I simply forgot with all that's been going on."

"That's understandable. We have been swamped. I think the book tour will be good for you, I really do. I can't do this alone, though, so I guess we'll just have to put things off for a little while. When does it start?"

"Next Monday through Friday. I'll be hitting local bookstores first and then doing day trips from the house. By Wednesday, I'll be out of town."

"That's fine dear, really. I could use a vacation from all of this anyway."

"Well, about that. How do you feel about John filling in for me?"

"Your husband? But he doesn't have any experience."

"Neither did we when we started out, right? Besides, he's been studying the equipment and knows more about it than I did when I started out."

"What about the kids?"

"Mom can watch them. He wouldn't be able to do it every night, but he could take up some of the slack while I'm gone."

"Is John alright... at his job I mean?"

"He missed the first round of layoffs, but they've cut back his hours."

"Sure, Amanda, that's fine. Tell him I said welcome aboard."

"Thanks, Mike. Oh, hey, that's my publisher on the cell phone. I've gotta run."

This particular turn of events turned over in Mike's mind as he ate his scrambled eggs. Bringing in John may turn out to be a blessing in disguise. He had grown weary of the work, and he thought this may actually be his way out. It wasn't that didn't enjoy what he was doing, so long as it could be taken in moderation. The more he thought about it, the more he warmed to the idea of bringing in a third, perhaps his replacement.

Chapter twelve

Due to the enormous success of their premier weekend event, Miller's Ferry opted to make Open Haunted Houses a weekly event on Fridays and Saturdays. As with any flavor of the month, their highpoint was at the outset, with a more manageable attendance settling in as a matter of course. What was feared to be a novelty wound up becoming a consistent, but modest industry throughout the rest of the season. Profits were always high, with many visitors returning a third or fourth time. Three new businesses opened on Main Street, and what few houses were for sale in the Historic District sold well above market value, and seventeen additional families now claimed the Miller's Ferry zip code as their own.

Amanda and the professor continued their work, along with their trusty apprentice, Amanda's husband John. With the majority of the houses in town now investigated and placarded, their schedule had eased up considerably. Much to their surprise, quite a few past customers were calling them back to re-investigate. Some of the houses had originally had nothing beyond explanation, but they were looking for a do-over. To nobody's surprise, nothing was to be found again. What was interesting to Mike and Amanda, was that during many of their return investigations, they were seeing far more activity than they had seen previously. The idea that Miller's Ferry was becoming more haunted was becoming increasingly apparent.

Itchy shut down his business for a week to redecorate and now ran an elegant, Victorian-style billiard parlor. Serving nothing but coffee and pastries, his establishment had grown into the kind of Bohemian hangout he and Leonard had discussed over coffee cups of Kentucky's Finest months earlier. Snooker and straight billiards were the preferred games now, but what people came for from miles around was a unique place to listen to good music and poetry readings while drinking the finest gourmet coffee in southwest Ohio. Itchy had all but lost his old clientele, but he had managed to work his way into a position of respect—perhaps even envy—within the rest of the community.

As with the citizenry, the ghosts of Haunted Miller's Ferry stratified into various castes. Pamela's murdered housewife was the star of the town, followed by the displaced spirits of several children. Jake Hauer's Civil War soldier ghost was always popular, and the emergence of a village founding father in one of the newly placarded houses was showing some real promise. Although many of the ghosts were not as interesting as the stars, they made a good second choice when the lines at the preferred houses were too long. Although there were only a few confirmed sightings of these spirits, the homeowners did such a good job in creating an atmosphere for a possible sighting that nobody left unsatisfied. Many, in fact, returned to improve their odds of an actual sighting.

The village was now gearing up for what would promise to be their biggest weekend: Halloween. The new gift shop on Main Street took deliveries all week in preparation for the event. The restaurants—including the new Italian Trattoria—decorated their dining rooms with appropriate décor and dressed their wait staff in period costumes similar to those of the placarded homeowners. The new bed and breakfast was booked solid for the whole weekend, with a long list of people hopeful for any cancellation. The two bars in town were now three, and all of them served the newly created mixed drink dubbed 'High Spirits,' the unofficial cocktail of Miller's Ferry.

Mike Pennington and Amanda elected to take the weekend off. While John and Amanda planned a weekend full of things to do with their kids, Mike had other plans. After he joined Madame Ovary on several of her jobs across the state, she finally consented to visit Miller's Ferry. Every placarded house that evening would be busy, so he opted to work in his own. The child long believed to dwell within his home had been confirmed by Amanda and him early on, but the only real evidence of that spectral child's existence was observed solely through their electronic eyes. He wanted to know more about the boy, so his house was as good as any other.

Madame Ovary arrived on time and made a grand entrance into Mike's home. Her appearance was reminiscent of a gypsy fortune teller, only toned down to more modest, basic colors.

"Madame Ovary, I am so glad you could make it. Please, come in."

"Hello, Mike. I think we're beyond formalities. Why don't you just call me Eunice?"

"Sure, Eunice. Here, let me take your coat." Mike helped her off with the garment, placing it in his hall closet, and then directed her to his sofa.

"So, tell me about your spirit. You said he is a child?"

"Yes. I believe his name is Charlie," he replied, taking a seat next to her. "In 1909, there was great flood that put this area under six feet of water. There were many deaths that year, and among them was Charlie, who was swept away by the flood waters."

"Have you interacted with him?"

"No. My partner and I registered him on a thermal imager, but that's about it."

"I see. Let's get right to it. Mike, close your eyes and relax yourself. Here... hold my hand."

He did as he was told and took Eunice's hand in his. It was warm and had a soft, tender feel to it. It had been a long time since he had touched a woman in such a familiar way, and it took him back to another place in time, when he was younger and more desirable. It was a happy feeling to have, and it began to awaken a long dormant desire. When she instructed him to clear his mind of all thoughts, he tried, but the lustful one stubbornly remained behind.

"I can feel a presence," she said, slowly and deliberately. "Yes, I can feel him. He is here with us. Charlie, is that you? It is Charlie. He is sad. He feels lost and alone. Charlie, I am calling another. Mary, have you found me? Ah, Mary. Tonight, we are with Charlie. See, Charlie? It's alright now. You're not alone anymore. Mary is going to take you somewhere. Go with her. Such a sweet child."

The conversation Eunice was having began to give Mike the chills. If she was a fraud, she was certainly a good one. There was an inexplicable, tingling energy he could feel enveloping them. Although he neither saw nor heard what she was experiencing, he could sense they were not alone.

After an extended period of silence, Eunice released her hand from Mike's and instructed him to open his eyes. "There," she said. "It is done."

"You've helped him to pass over?"

"That is up to him. I've given him over to my spirit guide, Mary. All she can do is lead him. Ultimately, it will be up to him what he does next."

"I see. So he may still want to hang around?"

"There are so many things I have yet to understand about the motives of spirits. Many of my peers have differing opinion.

Some feel they have to resolve what they left behind before they can cross over."

"Like Karma?"

"Exactly. Others feel that they are confused or lost and need to be led to the other side. I try to keep an open mind—as open as I can get in my profession. Many of the spirits I have helped do not return, but there are those who just don't want to go."

"This all seemed to be over rather quickly."

"Your spirit wanted to be reached. Tonight I made first contact, and I hope final. Helping them to cross over can take minutes, hours, even days. In some cases, I have to build an entire relationship with the spirit, and that takes time."

"I see. This is all very fascinating."

"And a little draining. Can I have something to drink?"

"Certainly. What would you like?"

"A beer would be fine."

Mike fled to the kitchen and returned with two bottles of beer.

Eunice took hers, thanking Mike in return. She removed a coaster from its caddy, and placed the bottle upon it on the coffee table in front of them. "So, Mike, tell me about yourself. How has your work been going?"

"I'll never be on your level, because my studies are more like field work. My partner and I are current on equipment and methodologies, and we have had tremendous success in verifying the existence of spirits in homes around town."

"Yes, you've been making quite a name for yourself, both in this world and the next."

"I always thought we were just a local institution."

"Mike, there are many who do what you do. They have a wide theatre of operations all over the country, limiting their activities to only a select few houses in any one location. What has been happening here in Pissquatta is rather a unique situation."

"Where did you get that name?"

"My spirit guide. Those with whom she has contact here call their town Pissquatta."

"We haven't called it by that name in a very long time."

"Yes, well, getting back to what I was saying, you have a very unique situation here."

"How so?"

"In that you have all made the spirits here into a cottage industry."

"Is that a bad thing?"

"It's hard to say. Many spirits enjoy the company of the living, while others will be angry at the intrusion into their afterlife."

"Before we started, sightings were a very rare experience."

"Indeed. Some feel their ability to reach out to us happens because of what is happening in their environment. They may develop the ability to manifest themselves when the air is charged in a lightning storm, or if there is a fast-flowing river or highway nearby."

"We have neither here."

"Through your search for the truth, Mike, you have created a different kind of energy in this town, fueled by its residents and visitors."

"So I have been making this town more haunted?"

"I believe so, yes."

"Well, then I have to stop."

"That would be like trying to fix the dam after it has burst. What's done is done."

"Can't we help them? The spirits, I mean."

"Like I said, some want to be helped, like your little boy here tonight. There are those who are quite content to stay. There is no telling what they want and no making them do what they wish not to do."

"So what *should* we be doing?"

"Time will tell, and then you will deal with it on a case-by-case basis. I would expect your job will become increasingly interesting."

"My God, it's Halloween. The town will be packed tonight with more expectant people than we've ever had."

"Yes, it should prove to be a very interesting night."

"Oh, Jimmy, let's go in this one."

"Come on. This one is lame. Says here he ran the livery. I want to go see the murdered housewife."

"The line is so long. It'll be at least an hour before we get into that one. Look, it's right here, and it's starting to get late."

"Fine. We'll go see the livery guy."

The intrepid couple entered though the front door of the Hoffler house and announced themselves. Although it had been a particularly busy night where the Hofflers were concerned, the crowds had tapered off about an hour earlier, and this couple was going to be their last before closing up for the night.

Robert and Ernie were costumed accordingly, but only Ernie dealt with the visitors. Robert cared little for the events—only the money, which he insisted the young couple immediately place in the urn by the door. He sat in the living room reading a newspaper, wearing his signature grave expression of discontent.

"Welcome to the Hoffler house," said Ernie, meeting his visitors in the front parlor. "I am Ernest Hoffler, and that surly-looking man over there is my brother Robert. How do you do?" Before the couple could respond, Ernie launched right into his spiel. "The Hoffler house has been in our family since 1832. My brother and I are both descendents of the original family that owned this house. We were investigated by SI earlier this year, and we believe our ghost is Thomas Hoffler, who settled here the year this house was built. He was a man of means, a tobacco merchant, who also owned the village livery."

"How did Thomas die, Mr. Hoffler?" asked the young woman.

"Well, the records from that era were a bit muddled, but as best as we can tell, he took his own life."

"Oh, how tragic."

As Ernie wound up for the next part of his address, the room became noticeably colder. Around them, the lights dimmed, and there arose a low mumbling sound. Standing next to Ernie, who was facing the couple, a shadow began to materialize. Initially, it was only the suggestion of a shadow—more like an area that lacked a little light. The couple grabbed each other's arms and pulled tightly together. Ernie, now noticing the apparition for the first time, stepped back as it materialized into the form of a man.

It reached out to the woman, making barely audible utterances. Eventually, it clearly and audibly said, "Josephine."

"My God!" gasped the young man.

"Josephine, why?" the apparition continued.

"What is this?" grumbled Robert, shuffling out of the living room, supported by his cane. "Holy shit! What the hell is that?"

"Josephine, why?" the apparition continued.

"I'm sorry! My name isn't Josephine," said the young woman by way of explanation. "Who is Josephine?"

"Josephine, why? Why didn't you leave your husband for me? We loved each other. You told me you would leave him. Why, Josephine, why?"

"I'm sorry. I don't understand."

"If I can't have you, nobody can. I will kill us both."

"Oh, I get it now. So you were banging Josephine Himmel next door?" explained Robert callously.

"What?" asked his brother Ernie.

"Josephine Himmel is the name of the murdered housewife at Pamela Holcum's house."

"No way! That can't be. The timeline is all off. Thomas killed himself a good five years after the murder, and the crime was never solved."

"I guess it is now," said the young man, who had found the presence of mind to start taking a video of the apparition.

"Why? Josephine, why? Why... why?"

As the spirit came, so did it leave: fading into wisps of shadowy smoke and then nothing.

"A murdering lover trumps a murdered housewife any day of the week," said Robert, breaking out into a thick smile. "We're going to be rich."

CHAPTER THIRTEEN

Leonard strolled into his office early Monday morning, without the benefit of a breakfast at the Ferry Crossing. He had cut back on much of his social networking as of late and enjoyed the solitary existence of work and home. It was unfortunate he did not pay a visit to the restaurant that morning, for if he had, he might have been better prepared for his day.

Lori rose from her desk as he entered the outer office. She had a concerned look on her face and a stack messages in her hand. "You didn't go to the Crossing this morning?"

"No, why?"

"Then I take it you don't know?"

"Know what? What's this all about, Lori?"

"Len, people have been calling all morning about what happened this weekend."

"What happened? Come on, now. I was away yesterday."

"Your ghosts."

"My ghosts?"

"All over town, there have been encounters with ghosts, and not all of them the friendly Casper kind. Here… these messages are just from this morning."

Leonard stepped up to Lori's desk and took the stack. As he thumbed through them, he read in disbelief about ghost sightings from all over town. If it were one or two, he would have quickly dismissed them, but there were far too many to dismiss as hopeful imaginings. "Thank you, Lori. I'll be in my office."

Leonard hung his coat by the door and sat behind his desk to better scrutinize the content of the messages. Before he could start, his phone rang with Pamela's number displayed on the caller ID. He sighed deeply and picked it up. "Good morning, Pamela. How can I help you today?"

"Good morning, Len. I've been talking to my ghost."

"Is that so? The murdered housewife, right? What did she have to say?"

"I'm glad you asked. She said the road outside of my house—our house—is the worst it has been in 100 years. You hear that, Len? Even the ghosts think you need to repave Oak Street."

"Thank you, Pamela. I'll take this under advisement."

"The village is getting some money back into its war chest. When do you think they can get to my street?"

"In the spring. It's getting too cold to pave asphalt now. I assure you, Pam, your street is the next to be done, and on that you have my solemn promise."

"I guess I'll have to settle for that, but I can't speak for my ghost. She says she wants to attend the next town hall meeting."

"That's fine, Pam. I'll see you both at the next—" but before he could answer, he heard the abrupt click that indicated the close of their conversation.

Just as he cradled the handset, the phone rang again. "Mayor Grey. How can I help you?"

"Mr. Mayor, this Janet Myles over on First Street. I have a ghost... I mean I know I have a ghost. My house was investigated."

"Yes. What is the problem?"

"I can see my ghost now. It was one thing for him to be here... but not be here. I saw him last night. I really saw him!"

"Oh really? Did he say anything?"

"No. He just stared at me with a funny-looking smile… while I was getting undressed," she continued in a hoarse whisper.

"Did you try going to a different room?"

"Yes. I locked myself in the bathroom, but he followed me in there. I didn't like the look he was giving me, like he expected me to give up my goodies."

"I see. This sounds serious."

"It is. I don't want to give up my goodies to some stranger, especially not to some dirty old ghost."

"Has he harmed you in any way?" Len asked, trying to sound serious and concerned but knowing full well that he was going to burst into boyish laughter if she said the word 'goodies' once more.

"No, I'm not sure he can."

"Well then, what do you want me to do?"

"I don't know. Make him stop?"

"That might be a tough one, Janet. Let me look further into this and get back to you."

Ring!

"Hello. Mayor Grey, how can I help you?"

"Mr. Mayor? This is Robert Johnson."

"The famous blues musician?"

"No relation. Listen, I just wanted to call you and thank you for all your fine work. I got the zoning back in the very beginning. In fact, I think I'm number three. Anyway, this has been an amazing experience. I met my ghost for the first time this weekend, and we've bonded."

"Well, I'm happy for you."

"My wife can't stand him. She says he's got a crude sense of humor. Personally, I like the guy. I think he's funny. Anyway, thanks. Bye."

Ring! Ring!

"Mayor Grey. How can I help you?"

"You're a bum, the worst thing that ever happened to this town. You should be impeached!"

"Is there anything else?"

"No, that should do it. Have a good one, Len. Bye."

Ring! Ring! Ring!

"Mayor Grey. How can I—"

"Mr. Mayor, I have a real honest-to-goodness ghost in my living room. I see him. I even got some pictures of him."

"Really? That's wonderful. Who is this?"

"Oh, I'm sorry. This is Emma Thompson. Remember me? I used to watch you when you were a little boy."

"Oh, hello, Emma. I could never forget you. How are you today?"

"Hello, I'm fine. The arthritis is acting up a bit, but otherwise I'm fine. I was so excited to see my ghost that I just had to call somebody."

"That's swell, Emma, and thanks for your call. Listen, I have to take another call. Are you going to be alright?"

"Oh, I'm fine. We've been sitting here watching the TV together. Do you watch the TV, Leonard?"

"No, not much. Listen, it's been great talking to you but—"

"He is the nicest man, very attentive. His name is Michael."

"Michael? That's great. Why don't I let you get back to watching TV then Emma?"

"Oh sure. I think I will. Goodbye, Leonard, and thanks for calling."

Before he even had time to breathe, another line lit up.

"Mayor Grey. How can I help you?"

"My house is haunted—I mean really haunted. Listen, I didn't know what I was getting into. If I were to get my house un-zoned, would that make the ghost go away?"

And so it went for the rest of the day. After the first three hours, Leonard conducted the rest of his calls over the speakerphone to give his aching ear a rest. The callers ranged from adulation to contempt, with little in between. There were those who were unsettled over the prospect of having to share their abode with their respective spectral cash-cows and those that were tickled silly over the novelty of their new netherworld friends.

Never in his wildest imagination had Leonard considered there might really be such things as ghosts. In only one afternoon, he went from a doubting Thomas to a true believer. Ordinarily, he had contingencies in place for almost any scenario, but this one required the skill and expertise of someone more familiar with the dark place in which he now found himself.

"Mike, I am in way over my head."

Mike came into his own living room from the kitchen with two cold beers, handing one to his best friend. Leonard took a sip and tried putting it on the coffee table, only to be intercepted by Mike and a coaster. "I must confess I never saw this one coming either. Have you seen your own ghost at home?"

"No, nothing. Why not?"

"I had Madame Ovary—I mean Eunice—over here the other night."

"Ordinarily, I'd crack some kind of joke, but I'm listening."

"Usually, most people don't have the capacity to see these apparitions, except perhaps for small children and pets. She seems to feel our spirits here in Miller's Ferry are soaking up energy to manifest themselves in ways they ordinarily could not. She thinks it all began with our initial investigations, and reached a head when we opened the houses to a waiting public with an honest belief in their presence and a desire to see them."

"I guess that's as good an explanation as any. Since no one has toured my house, it's unlikely she would be able to show herself. How many more houses are on your list for investigation?"

"Fifteen, but only four of them are for an original investigation. Of those four, three have already cancelled after hearing the news of what happened this weekend. As far as the repeat customers, about half have changed their minds and want their ghosts evicted."

"Can you do that? Is it like some kind of exorcist thing?"

"It can be done, under some circumstances. Eunice helped my spirit to cross over."

"Really? You got rid of your ghost?"

"She did it the night before last."

"You think she could do it for other people here in town?"

"She anticipated something might happen Halloween night, and I think she will be open to an invitation to do some work."

"So, uh, her calling on you the other night… just business?"

Mike tried diverting his attention to anything else in the room. "Ya got me, Len. We're an item," he replied with a sheepish grin.

"You old dog. Did you have to resort to your old tactics of plying her with alcohol before taking advantage of her?"

"More like the other way around."

"Ha, ha, ha! Mike, you kill me. Did she spend the night?"

"Leonard, I am surprised at you for asking such a question. I will not dignify that with a response… but we did have breakfast in our pajamas."

"You and Madame Ovary, huh? This has been a strange year for us, old friend."

"It has indeed, and I have the feeling it is about to get much stranger. Say, what's that going on next door at your place?"

Leonard followed Mike's gaze out the side window to the front of his house. Two vans and several cars were parked out front on the street, with people busily bustling about in his front yard. The two men got up from the couch, walking out through the front door and out onto Mike's front yard.

"What is this?" asked Leonard, scratching his head.

"That, my friend, is your fifteen minutes of fame. Those are TV news crews."

"Don't that beat all?"

"Look! There's Susan Balsom, the buxom blonde of Channel Seven, right there at your front door. Uh oh! I think they've made us."

"I'm not ready for this. I never thought we'd get this far," said Leonard apprehensively.

The crowd of reporters and camera personnel moved en masse from Leonard's yard into Mike's. Within seconds, the two men were drenched in light and drowning in a sea of microphones stabbing at their faces.

"Mr. Mayor, Susan Balsom with the Channel Seven news team, the number one news team in the tri-state area. Startling videos have exploded the ghost sensation of your town on the internet. Are we looking at an elaborate hoax or 'the most haunted town in Ohio,' as you have claimed?"

"Hi, Susan. First, I would like to thank you for your interest in our little village. Miller's Ferry, a strategically situated bedroom community to the great city of Cincinnati, is foremost and utmost a community steeped in tradition and values. As one of Ohio's oldest communities, we have a long and rich history. We value God, family, and community. It is the kind of special place you want to raise your kids and live your life in the way it was meant to be enjoyed. We, the folks of Miller's Ferry, do not pretend to be anything other than the good people we say we are. The stories you have been hearing and the videos you have seen are quite real."

"Yes, but 'the most haunted town in Ohio'? How do you make such a claim?"

"Until someone comes along to prove otherwise, it is a claim I stand behind. Can you prove we are not the most haunted town in Ohio?'

"And you, sir, you are Mike Pennington of Spectral Investigators, correct?"

"I am."

"So you have been conducting the investigations into paranormal activity for this town?"

"I have."

"What is your background in this sort of work?"

"Well, I—"

Leonard leaned forward to the microphone to cut off his friend. "Professor Pennington is an acclaimed academic and paranormal enthusiast. He uses state-of-the-art equipment and modern investigative techniques, while conducting all of his investigations with the utmost integrity."

"Are all the houses that you are paid to investigate haunted?"

"No," replied Mike flatly.

"What the professor means is that not every house has a spectral anomaly that defies explanation."

"What I mean," continued Mike, interrupting Leonard's interruption, "is that just because I have been hired to investigate a house, there is no guarantee I will find anything. My partner—"

"His SI partner, Amanda Bremner, is the author of Haunted Miller's Ferry, available at your nearest bookstore," added Leonard, always happy to do some marketing.

"My partner and I have conducted many investigations in this town, many producing remarkable and very convincing evidence of paranormal activity. We have also found that quite a few houses had absolutely nothing in them that could not be explained. I hope you weren't implying we are in the business of selling ghosts."

"Just trying to get the facts straight, Professor," replied Susan.

"Mr. Mayor, Edward O'Neal from your old paper."

"Eddy, is that you?" replied Leonard, shielding his eyes from the bright lights to connect the voice with a familiar face in the back of the crowd. "I see you finally made it out of obituaries. Good for you."

"Thanks, Len. Mr. Mayor, this reporter has heard allegations that your administration has been remiss in effecting infrastructure improvements to the village. Any comment?"

Without any doubt in his mind, he knew Pamela Holcum was behind the allegations. "It's all true, Eddy. Miller's Ferry has not been immune to this recession, and capital improvements took a big hit."

"I couldn't help but notice your street is looking pretty nice."

"The timing for that improvement last year was simply a coincidence, and other areas have unfortunately had to wait. Like I was saying, we have seen hard times, but we have really been able to turn that around for the better. For instance, I will be meeting with the city manager tomorrow to discuss the repaving of Oak Street in the spring, along with a few other streets. Miller's Ferry is a village on the move—the kind of town that takes care of its own."

"Professor, David Jenkins from Channel Two news, with the widest coverage of Doppler Radar in the tri-state area. You talked about 'investigation' and 'evidence.' Are you willing to share your findings with the public?"

"Certainly, as long I have the homeowners' consent. I am more than willing to offer full disclosure."

"Like I said before," continued Leonard, "we are a community with values and integrity. Nobody is trying to get one over on you. We'll be having another Open House next weekend, and I encourage you all to come on down and judge the facts for yourself."

"Hello, this is Joey of Ghost Investigators. How can I help you."

"Joey, it's Al. Did you check out those internet links I sent you last night?"

"Yeah, I sure did. Ow!"

"What are you doing?"

"Running electrical conduit. What are you doing?"

"I don't have a day job, remember?"

"Right, so that means you're in your mom's basement, drinking beer and shopping online."

"Wrong. It means I have found us another job. We're going to Miller's Ferry, Ohio."

"Kind of figured that. Where does that guy get off saying they are the most haunted town in Ohio? We already proved that's Athens. We even have a show on cable. Does he? Man, I really do not want to go back to Ohio. I thought you were working on getting us a job in Tuscon?"

"Yeah. I already got that one, but I pushed it back a couple of weeks. C'mon, man. This is a personal challenge now. We have to prove them wrong or eat crow."

"Fine. So we'll go back to Ohio. Tell me about the job."

"Nineteenth-century home, the ghost is believed to be that of a murdered housewife, caught up in an affair that ended with murder/suicide."

"Sounds juicy. Okay, so let's make it happen. Go ahead and contact the network to set up a camera crew. As soon as I finish this job, I'll call the rest of the team in. Looks like we're heading back to Ohio."

CHAPTER FOURTEEN

Leonard hadn't paid a visit to Itchy's since his grand re-opening. By distancing himself from his pulse points, he had neglected some of his friendships, and this wore at his conscience. The old truck was in a good mood that day, so he rambled, shook, and jarred his way on over to the new Itchy's Billiard Parlor.

Although the front essentially appeared to be the same through the new coat of paint, the inside was another matter. The familiar bell that tinkled upon entering the establishment had been replaced with an electronic eye that sounded a silent alarm, probably back in the office. The time-worn plank floor was now covered in stone tile. The old standard pool hall tables were gone, replaced by mahogany tables, richly adorned with carved features and covered in red felt instead of green. They were fewer in number to leave room for additional cocktail tables and chairs, the kind one might find in a Parisian sidewalk café. There were now a stage with lights and a large barista counter in the back.

"I was beginning to wonder if I'd ever see you in here again, Len."

"Hiya, Itch. I like what you've done with the place. One thing though. What's that smell?"

"Smell? What smell?"

"Exactly."

"Oh, my new clientele won't abide smoking. Customer's always right, you know. Buy you a cup coffee?"

"Sure," replied Leonard, following Itchy into the back office.

The office had escaped the hands of the decorators and continued to hold its valued place in time. Leonard took a seat on the old sofa, while Itchy fumbled about the same old trusty office coffee maker.

"You aren't actually pouring me coffee, are you? A little bourbon would be nice."

"Don't drink bourbon no more, Mr. Mayor, but perhaps I can interest you in two fingers of eighteen-year-old scotch," replied Itchy, turning around with a tumbler of the fine liquor and handing it Leonard.

"Oh, only if you insist. Thanks." Leonard took a sip. "Oh, is that good."

Itchy took up his own glass and headed around to his chair behind the desk. Once he had propped his feet up, he took a sip and sighed with great satisfaction.

"Where is everyone, Itchy?"

"The old crowd don't come 'round here no more."

"Why's that?"

"Too many changes is all I can figure. I guess since there ain't no more pulse for you to take here, so you'll be shying away too?"

"I thought you knew me better than that, Itch. We go back way too far. Hell, I remember when you were still called 'James'."

"Different time, different man. What am I saying? I'm a different man than I was just last year."

"I never thought I'd see you wearing a jacket and a collared shirt."

"Sleeveless Harley t-shirts just don't go with the new customer base. Like Dylan said, 'Times, they are a-changin,' and

I'm changing with them," he replied, tucking his tweed jacket sleeve into his side pocket

"You ever miss the old pool hall?"

"Sure I do, but the money is just too damned good to get all teary eyed."

"Seems to be a lot of that going around."

The conversation hung at that last revelation for a long, thoughtful moment.

"It's a good thing," replied Itchy. "It's what we all want, even if things are getting a little weird."

"Oh, you mean the ghosts?"

"Never thought there were such things. Who'd a'thunk it? What I'm talking 'bout, though, is more weirdness."

"I didn't think it could get any weirder."

"The town is changing, Len, and so are the people. Did you know we now have minorities?"

"C'mon now, Itch, I thought you were a better man than that."

"I don't begrudge no one, but there are those who will be just a little uncomfortable knowing there are now gay couples living in town."

"Really? Who?"

"That old house that sold on Elm Street."

"Oh come on! That guy can't be gay. He's a lawyer."

"Yep, and his partner is an engineer. I'm telling you, like three-dollar bills. Also have a couple lesbian witches that moved in on Arch Street."

"Witches? You mean with broomsticks and pointy hats and all?"

"Actually, I think they prefer to be called Wiccan. And there's a new couple, this man and woman who walk a big wolf around town."

"I've seen them, and that can't be a wolf."

"It's a wolf, Len. Rumors are flyin' around they are devil worshipers."

"Because they have a wolf?"

"You know how rumors go."

"My, my, aren't we becoming urban?"

"Like I said, friend, different time, different place."

Leonard sipped on his scotch and rolled the new information around in his head. "It's a good thing really. We could use a little diversity."

"I think it's a fine thing. They're all good paying customers of mine. You know, Leonard, the way things are going, you may be getting a whole new pulse point to monitor."

"I wonder how the village-Herberts are going to take it?"

"What the hell have you done to our town, you jackass?" demanded Herb Schlemmer as Leonard walked into Richard's Barbershop.

"Good morning, Herb. Good to see you. Hi, fellas," Leonard continued, acknowledging Herb's fellow Masons, lined up in chairs next to him across the wall.

"Don't think you can hustle my vote anymore—or anyone else's I know, for that matter. I don't recognize this place anymore. Have you seen what's moved in? Well, have you? Queers," he finished in a whisper.

"What's the matter, Herb? Do they challenge your masculinity?"

Richard's three sages, who sat apart from Herb and his entourage, snickered at Leonard's retort.

"What are you three girls laughing at?" snapped Herb "They'll bring down your property values too."

"Herbert, do us a favor and shut the hell up," replied George Schuler. "You don't speak for the rest of us, and I would thank you to lay off the queer comments. Would it surprise you to know my son is gay?"

The two other sages raised their eyebrows in surprise to this proclamation.

"Do you really think I'm going to love him any less because of his choice in lifestyle?"

"Your son's gay, George?" asked Arthur Benze. "You never told us that."

"Never felt I had to. Why?"

"Well, I was just wondering, is he a beer-drinking man or a wine-sipping man?"

"He's an auto worker and a proud beer-drinking man."

"Yeah, but how about his partner?" asked Ryan. "Beer or wine?"

"He's an iron worker and a beer drinker too."

"Yes, but do you think he drinks wine at home?" continued Arthur.

"Do you guys have any idea how hard it was for him to come out of the closet to me? He ain't secretly drinking wine, trust me."

"You guys are idiots, you know that?" boomed Herb. His two fellow Masons nodded with the appropriate amount of disdain. "You may think it's alright, but I—"

"Oh, here it comes," said Leonard

"I think it's an abomination against God. There's a special place in hell for guys like that. You should do your son a favor and get him right."

With this, all conversation and activity came to an abrupt halt. Richard's scissors stopped mid-snip, while his uncomfortable customer stared slack jawed at Herb. Ordinarily, Richard had little to say, save the small talk a barber engages in with his customers. He put the scissors down on the counter and turned back to face Herb. "Herbert, your business is no longer welcome here. I do not like you or men who are like you. Please leave my establishment."

"You're kidding, right? Come on, Richard! You've always cut my hair."

"Do you really want your hair cut by a queer?"

"Wow," said Leonard, chuckling. "Now that's a bombshell."

"This is a Goddamned conspiracy," grumbled Herb, who stood up quickly, his two minions following suit. "This is all your fault, Grey. Everything was just fine until you came up with your stupid ghost idea."

"Apparently, it wasn't. The world is changing, Herb, whether you like it or not. The town you thought you once knew was just a veneer, and this town is going to become a smaller place for guys with your narrow-minded views."

"The town I once knew is dead. Come on, fellas. Let's get out of here."

The three men left the barbershop with their heads up and their opinions intact. The door slammed behind them, echoing off the walls of the silent shop.

"You're really gay, Richard?" asked George. "Are you a wine drinker or a beer drinker?"

Pastor Cheryl spent her weekdays in her church office, busily attending to the myriad of clergy jobs that generally go unnoticed by all. She was active within her community and her congregation and wasted little in the way of time during normal working hours. She sat at her desk working on her calendar, scheduling visits with various shut-ins, when she heard a knock on her open door. "Well, hello, Leonard. What brings you down here?"

"I couldn't help but notice your sign out front of the church, 'Guaranteed Ghost this Sunday'. I don't believe you ever got certified, did you?"

"Since when do I need a certificate for the Holy Ghost?"

"Ahh," laughed Leonard. "Not bad."

"Well, I need a hook too. Please, sit down. Now, what's on your mind?"

"Do you ever feel like you wish you could turn back time?"

"I think everyone gets to that place eventually. I try to live following my heart, living without regrets. I may not always be right, but I am always true to myself and those around me."

"Maybe that's my problem. I tend to think too much."

"Is that how you feel? Shame on you, Leonard Grey. I have to admit this ghost business has been a little unsettling for me, but what you did, you did for the town. Rarely have I met so selfless a man as Mayor Leonard Grey."

"Thanks, Cheryl, but I'm beginning to have second thoughts about the whole thing."

"What on Earth for?"

"Where do I begin? For starters, it seems I've inadvertently raised the dead and driven a wedge between members of the community."

"First of all, only one man rose from the dead where you're concerned. As far as these alleged ghost sightings, I haven't seen any myself, so I'm really not sure how to comment on that. I will say, though, that from everything I've heard so far, they've always been around here, and you have finally given them a voice."

"Maybe, but it's a voice many don't want to hear. That one I think I can fix, but it's what I'm doing to this community that bothers me. I just got into it with a fella over this. It's not that I mind if he doesn't like me. I've got broad shoulders and a thick skin for that sort of thing. What bothers me is how men like him think, especially where some of our new residents are concerned. Had I not done any of this and just let the town go on the way it was, that kind of hatred would never have been brought to a boil."

"I think I know what you're talking about, Leonard. Now, I want you to listen to me, very closely. Towns like this are slow to embrace change, but change is inevitable. Deal with it now, deal with later, but sooner or later people will have to deal with it."

"I ended up making a man come out of the closet today. I hate to think what it is going to do to his business."

"Nobody made him do that. Nothing stifles the soul more than living with an unbearable lie, so I would imagine what he said gave him tremendous relief. I can't tell you how people are going to respond to that news, but sooner or later, he was going to have deal with it. Hmm... 'Deal With It'... I think I have the beginnings of a sermon."

"How do you think we're doing, Cheryl?"

"I suppose things are going well, and for the record, things have been pretty good for the church lately. These ghostly encounters have brought people to a place in their lives where the divine is not such an abstract idea. The pews have been filling, the collections are up, and many people in this town are considering their own mortality for the first time in their lives. It's one thing to show up here every Sunday and try to buy your salvation through attendance, but it's quite another to truly contemplate the infinite."

"So it's been a good thing, right?"

"It's been a good thing, Leonard," replied Cheryl, smiling.

"Here, Len," said Mike, passing him a beer from the fridge. "Tell me about your day."

"You were right about things getting stranger," replied Leonard, leaning up against Mike's kitchen counter. "Started the day off visiting Itchy."

"How is the town's favorite one-arm bandit doing these days?"

"I hardly recognized him. He's gone from a boozing pool shark to a herringbone tweed scotch sipper."

"No kidding?"

"You see his new place yet? It's incredible. It's more of a beatnik coffee house than what it used to be. Oh, I suppose in many ways, he's still the same man underneath it all, but still… he has changed."

"Did you ever stop to consider he has become the man he always wanted to be?"

"Now that's why I like hanging out with philosophy professors."

"And maybe you are becoming the man you were always meant to be. I find we are often defined by how we deal with the circumstances we get ourselves into."

"Funny you should say that. I really tripped Herbert's breaker today."

"I heard. What a horse's ass. You know what the real crime with him is?"

"Tell me."

"That he has been allowed to procreate."

"Nice one, Mike. So I guess you also heard about Richard?"

"I did. Tell me, you've known him a long time, right?"

"His whole life."

"Now that he's come out, do you feel any differently about him?"

"I can't say it makes a difference."

"That's exactly how all of his real friends will feel. Friendship is what defines a man."

"I thought circumstances defined a man?"

"Well that too. Plenty of things define a man. I really think I'm going to make a list someday."

"How are things going with the business?"

"Bad for the old business, good for the new. I've spent most of this week helping Eunice with spirit crossings."

"How many?"

"Nine so far, with more to follow."

"I can see the sense in culling some of the homes from the tour."

"I think after I'm finished, we'll have an acceptable balance."

"Pretty sweet deal, Mike. It's like you're getting paid at both ends."

"It wasn't supposed to be like that, but what can you do? I don't charge nearly as much for the crossings. We don't use any equipment, and Eunice does almost all of the work. All I get is a modest finder's fee."

"And Amanda?"

"Thankful for having a week off. Ever since last weekend, sales on her book have skyrocketed. She's busy doing signings and enjoying her celebrity status. Speaking of celebrities, guess who's coming to town?"

"I have no idea."

"The Ghost Investigators."

"Those guys on TV? *The Guys from GI?*"

"The very same. As it turns out, the Hofflers' ghost murdered Pamela's ghost amidst a torrid love affair. When Robert Hoffler started talking trash about Pamela's murdered housewife, Pamela upped the ante by contacting *The Guys from GI*. She's getting her ghost onto cable TV."

"What a resourceful woman. Honestly, she scares me sometimes."

"A lot of that had to do with yours truly."

"How so?"

"When she found out about the Hoffler's murderous lover ghost, she panicked over the prospect of losing business. She contacted me about providing testimony in a lawsuit against the Hofflers. I suggested she contact GI before going through with the suit, and they bit. Oh, by the way, they're coming to debunk your theory that Miller's Ferry is the most haunted town in Ohio."

"I say bring it!"

"They're also going to be challenging my findings," said Mike reluctantly.

"How do you feel about that?"

"Bring it!"

Chapter fifteen

The arrival of the Ghost Investigators that following Saturday was marked by the arrival of a procession of three black SUVs into the center of Miller's Ferry. They arrived at noon and parked along the street at the Ferry Crossing for lunch. As they stepped from their vehicles, they were immediately recognized as celebrities, and within minutes of being seated inside the restaurant, every other table was filled with fans eager to meet and talk to *The Guys from GI*.

After lunch, they politely bade everyone in the restaurant farewell and wended their way through town to Mike Pennington's house.

After polite introductions at the front door, Mike invited the team into his house, along with their extended camera crew. "I can't thank you guys enough for stopping by," gushed Mike. "I'm a big fan of your work."

"Yes, we understand you're in the trade as well."

"I am the town's resident investigator. My partner here, Amanda—"

"Hi," said Amanda with a broad grin.

"We've done all of the work here in town."

"Great, great. So let's get to it. We'd like to see some of your findings."

"Sure," said Mike obligingly. "We have terabytes of raw data, so Amanda and I have created a montage DVD of some of the more startling evidence."

The group sat down in Mike's living room, filling up the furniture and requiring additional chairs from the dining room. Amanda picked up the remote control and hit 'play' on the DVD player.

"Now, this was one hour, fifteen minutes into our fourth investigation. It was an 1860 house, with numerous sightings by the occupants. Coming in on the left of the frame is a ball of light... there it is."

"We pick up images like this often," said Joey, a little critically. "It could be attributed to suspended dust particles."

"That's what I thought at first, but have you ever seen dust do this?"

The ball of light stopped its journey across the frame, as if it had noticed the camera for the first time. It moved in on the lens, increasing in size through its proximity, until the screen was filled with a bright light, at which point the camera was knocked over.

"Oh, this is a good one. We were in the cellar of an 1872 house when we recorded this audio."

Amanda's voice: "Professor, I'm getting something over here."

Professor's voice: "Nothing on the camera... wait, listen."

Unidentified voice: "Mmm_ _ _ MMmm_ _ _pl_ _ _ _"

"We isolated the noise and got this."

Unidentified voice: "Mommy, Mommy, please."

"It's so clear. That one still gives me the shivers," said Amanda

The DVD played for about an hour, culminating in their shared experience in the 1840 house, where everyone in the room watched as a clearly defined figure on the infrared placed his hand upon Amanda's shoulder. Mike turned off the television and scanned the room for any response in the faces of his guests.

"Well?" he asked, fishing for anything.

"Well," began Joey under the watchful eye of his personal camera crew, "that's pretty incredible."

Mike sat back in his chair, relieved.

"Maybe a little too incredible."

"What do you mean?" asked Mike, sitting back up again.

"What I mean is we've been doing this kind of work all over the country in what are considered America's premier haunted houses, with numerous documented sightings. In all the time we've been doing this, we have never seen anything like what you have here."

"I'm not sure I understand what you're trying to say," replied Amanda, a little defensively.

"What I'm saying is I doubt the validity of your findings."

"Now see here," huffed Mike, standing up.

At the first sign of conflict, the cameras all swung around and focused on him.

"If you are calling us liars, you better have something to back that up."

"Settle down, Professor. We're not calling you liars, I just think your evidence may have been... uh, enhanced... to, uh... to better substantiate your findings."

"What you're trying to say is that we manufactured it, and with that, we are at odds."

"Hey, fellas," said Joey, turning to the crew, "turn off the cameras." The crew obliged and laid their equipment on the floor. "Listen, I'm at odds with some guy nobody has ever heard of, in a town nobody has ever heard of, coming up with stuff nobody has ever seen before. I'm sorry, but it's all just a little too fantastic."

"Who the hell do you think you are to question our work like that?"

"Who are we? We're the ones who are on TV every week. We have an audience, a fan base, and we're syndicated with spinoffs. Who the hell are you?"

"You've got a lot of nerve," interrupted Amanda. "When we first started out, you might have been able to bully us and pick apart our work, but we are not some fly-by-night operation looking to get on Youtube. We provide an open-minded investigative service to our customer base, and it comes with state-of-the-art equipment and considerable experience."

"Experience? What have you really got?"

"You want to talk numbers?" continued Amanda. "We've done more investigations in this town than you did in your whole first season. You think TV cameras give you the right to sit all high and mighty? You're an electrical contractor, I'm a housewife, and he's a retired philosophy teacher. I'd say it's a pretty level playing field where experience is concerned."

"Okay. Tempers are starting to flare, and I'm sorry if I've insulted you. Please sit down."

Mike and Amanda slowly sat down, still visibly irked at Joey's condescending comments.

"Try to see things from our perspective. We started out as bunch of ordinary guys, following our interest in investigating paranormal activities. This TV show has made us stars, and people see us now as the reigning authority on all things ghost. That isn't what we set out to achieve, but it is what it is. So, we go on national television to proclaim Athens as the most haunted town in Ohio, and then you guys come along and say we are wrong. Don't you think we might take that a little personally?"

"Joey, when Amanda and I first started this, it was to help out a friend who wanted to save his town. We didn't know the first thing about ghost investigating, so we modeled our business after yours. We used all of your protocols, bought the same equipment you use, and set out with the same objectivity you boast about on your show. It was never our intention to knock you down—only to flatter you through our imitation."

"But, Mike, nobody has ever seen the kind of things you showed us here today. I believe in all that we do, but if I could get footage like that, our ratings would go through the roof."

"We are not liars. Here… I'll say it again, just in case you missed it the first time. We-are-NOT-liars."

Joey looked back and forth between the professor and Amanda and then turned to his camera crew. "Alright, turn 'em back on."

The crew shouldered their equipment and focused back on everyone in the room.

Joey turned back to Mike and Amanda with a different perspective. "Now, tell me about the Holcum investigation."

As the last of the SUVs pulled away from Mike's house, Leonard emerged though his front door and caught Mike's attention, who was standing out on his front lawn watching the vehicles drive off. Mike beckoned him to come over as he walked back into his house.

"So how did it go?" asked Leonard, closing the front door behind him.

"I don't think I'll ever watch that show again," said Amanda with contempt.

"That good?"

"I thought they would try to explain away our findings," started Mike, "but they just flat out called us liars."

"How did you handle that one?"

"With my usual grace and charm. We were able to agree to disagree, but still, my ego took a bit of a bruising."

"That's alright, Mike," said Amanda "He's in for a big surprise at the Holcum house tonight."

"Is that a good haunted house?" asked Leonard.

"Sure," replied Mike, "probably the most active in town. Pamela gets the most visitors, and that only seems to feed her ghost. There have been many confirmed visual sightings and at least three interactions."

"I think her spirit is enjoying her notoriety," added Amanda. "You know, a woman's vanity?"

"These spirits aren't actually dangerous, are they?" asked Leonard.

"Can't say for sure," replied Mike. "So far, all of our encounters have been pretty benign, but we're still relatively new to the game."

"What does Madame Ovary think?"

"She told me she has run into a number of hostile ghosts, but she's still here."

"I suppose that's something. So what time do they start their investigation?"

"Lights out at nine o'clock."

"Will you two be joining them?"

"Nah. We are to sit this one out. They're concerned our presence in their investigation would be leading and biased."

"So how is that bad? You could lead them right up where you believe the ghost is."

"They need to draw their own conclusions, Len. If I were in their position, I'd probably make the same call."

"So what do you plan to do this evening?"

"I'm staying in, and Amanda is going home to be a mom and wife tonight. Feel like hanging out?"

"No thanks. I'm taking Bea up to the Stumble Inn."

"Ahh, a little dinner and perhaps some karaoke?"

"Sure. I'm going to try and wrangle a duet out of Belt Buckle Bob."

"That should be interesting. How are things with you and Bea?"

"Fine, fine. She's a fun girl, but I'm beginning to see some signs of power hunger within her."

"How so?"

"I caught her threatening one of the homeowners. Bea told her to support an agenda that is coming up in November or she would steer the walking tours past her house. Her Historical Society once used those kinds of tactics, and I think she sometimes longs for the old days."

"Old habits die hard, I guess. Did you set her straight?"

"Yeah. I guess I'm her voice of reason these days."

"You're a real Jiminy Cricket, Len."

"That's me, the moral standard of Miller's Ferry. Think I should put it on a business card?"

"A banner across Main Street should suffice."

"Well, I have to get going. Don't let those Guys from GI bully you none," said Leonard, turning to leave Mike and Amanda's company.

"Sure, Len, and good luck with Bob tonight," Mike replied as Leonard left through the front door.

"So, the mayor and Beatrice?" asked Amanda.

"Quite the item. It seems like it was just yesterday you and I dragged him down that road."

"Is he happy?"

"I think so, but it can be hard to get an accurate read on Leonard these days. He has evolved from everybody's friend and neighbor into quite the politician. Sometimes I fear I might lose him to this role he has cast for himself."

"Oh, I hope not."

"It's hard to say, Amanda. This little scheme of his has blown up into something much bigger than even he ever expected. Miller's Ferry is definitely on the move, and everything we ever knew or thought we knew about our little village is radically changing. If we are to survive all this, I suspect we will all have to change."

It had been two and a half hours since the lights went out in Pamela Holcom's house. She had been cast out with her husband prior to the investigation, giving The Guys from GI unfettered access to her domain. A blend of inquisitive fans and weekend visitors continued to assemble out on the sidewalk, curious as to what the team might find.

Joey and his partner climbed the narrow staircase to the second landing, followed by a camera operator. The streetlights outside filtered in through bedroom windows, eliminating any need for night vision gear. Upon giving each of the front bedrooms a thorough examination, they walked the hallway to the bedroom at the back of the house.

"So far it's been a bit of a bust," said Joey, peering into his camera viewer.

"It isn't helping that professor's credibility any."

"He seems like a nice guy. He really doesn't come off as a fraud, but then again, you just never know."

As they approached the closed door at the end of the hallway, the knob turned on its own, and it slowly swung open.

"Tell me that didn't just happen. Hello? Is anybody in there?" Joey cried out into the darkness."

"Come in. I've been waiting for you," came a feminine voice within.

Joey and Al looked at each for some explanation and then back at the doorway. Joey held his portable camera out in front of himself and followed it slowly into the room. Al stepped in behind and stopped next to Joey. The two stood motionless, looking beyond the camera viewer to something that lay beyond any of their explanations.

"Hello, gentlemen," greeted the shadowy apparition standing at the foot of the bed.

Mike lowered the volume on his television set and rose from his couch to answer the urgent banging at his front door. Upon opening it, he was surprised to see Leonard and Beatrice.

"Mike, they went packing… and I mean in a hurry."

"Leonard, Bea, please come in."

"Hello, Mike," answered Bea. "Sorry to bother you at this late hour, but there was no holding him back."

"Please sit down," Mike offered as they entered. He shut the door and followed them into the living room. "Now, what is this all about?"

"The Guys from GI," answered Leonard excitedly. "Whatever they saw must have scared them good, because they just tore out of town."

"Really? What happened?"

"Bea and I were up at the Stumble Inn—"

"Karaoke night," Bea chimed in. "You should have heard Bob and Leonard sing 'On the Road Again'!"

"Right," continued Leonard. "Anyway, while we were there, this guy runs in and yells that they had just finished their investigation and says they were leaving. Turns out, a bunch of people had been following this thing, so they all left at once to go down the block to Pamela's house. We decided to tag along and see what the fuss was about," he continued, sitting down on the sofa next to Bea.

"There really wasn't anybody left in the bar, so why not?" she added by way of explanation.

"By the time we got there, The Guys from GI were throwing their stuff into one of the SUVs, literally throwing it. Big tangled balls of cable, their equipment, the boxes for the equipment—they were just throwing it."

"It really was quite disorganized, Mike."

"Anyway, this guy who had been outside the whole time said the two stars came running out of that house like they were being chased by Beelzebub himself. Didn't say anything to anybody except 'Come on! We got to get out of here!' Their cameraman dropped his camera on the sidewalk when he came running out."

"No way!" said Mike, taking up a seat in his chair. "What a bunch of pansies."

"Whatever happened to them in there scared the shit of them. Oops... sorry, Bea."

"That's okay, dear. I would have said the same thing."

"Seems to me someone owes you a big apology, Mike."

"Don't that beat all?" replied Mike with a big, satisfied grin. "Looks like your little town here is going to get some national coverage."

Leonard's enthusiasm suddenly disappeared at Mike's revelation. He sat back and clasped his hands in his lap. "I don't think that's what I want at all."

"I thought recognition was a good thing?"

"It is, but too much of it is a bad thing. You've seen what this has been like lately. It get's crazy enough just with a local crowd. The last thing I want is to be some kind of national shrine."

"Oh, he's right about that," said Bea. "There's never parking in town anymore, and the visitors always leave such a mess."

"I see your point," replied Mike. "Hold on a sec. Joey gave me his business card. Let me see if his cell phone number is on it." Mike got up from his chair and went over to his desk. He rummaged through piles of paper and desk debris until he found it. He hammered out the number on his phone and waited for an answer.

"Hello? This is Joey."

"Joey, Professor Pennington here. How are you?"

"I am so sorry. I take back everything I said about you and your partner."

"Really? What did you see?"

"We saw the ghost… really saw the ghost. I'm sure we have some fantastic footage of it too."

"Did you have an interaction?"

"Interaction? She hit on me."

"You're kidding!"

"No, I'm not kidding. Plain as day, she stood there ogling at me and asked how long I was in town for. I didn't know what to do or what to say. I just stood there like a deer caught in the high beams. So then she comes over and tries to pinch my ass."

"Did you feel something?"

"Yeah, a weird tingling sensation. To tell you the truth, it felt kind of good, but at the same time, scary as hell."

"What did you do next?"

"Ran! We all ran as fast we could. That's the fastest we ever did a demobilization on any site. Professor, I've never experienced anything like that before. I still don't know what to think about it."

"So when do you think it will air?"

"Never."

"Why is that?"

"If that goes on TV, people will say the same thing about me that I said about you, and our credibility will go right out the window. Maybe between seasons we'll come back to do some more work with you and Amanda, but this one will go into my private library."

"I see. Well don't let me hold you up anymore. You be safe."

"Thanks, Mike." Mike lowered the phone down, back into its cradle. He turned to Leonard and Bea, perched at the edge of the couch like expectant grandparents, waiting for the news from the hospital.

"Well?" asked Leonard.

"Well, I don't think you'll have to worry about any new people."

Chapter sixteen

In the following months, the weather grew colder, the foot traffic lessoned, and the paranormal activity fell into a welcomed lull. Everyone in town was quietly thankful for the decline in business, for after the news of The Guys from GI running as fast as their SUVs could carry them out of town was posted on the local blogs, interest in the little town dramatically spiked. The immediate new wave of Spectral Enthusiast, as they had come to be dubbed, was not as much of a strain on the little community as Mayor Leonard Grey had feared, but it had become a bit of a nuisance. The police were constantly following up on reports of missing lawn ornaments, house plaques, and even mailboxes that had been taken as souvenirs by devoted fans of the haunted village.

Financially, the past year had proven to be a profound windfall for all. The community as whole enjoyed the benefits of the new wealth, with the following tax season promising to take them within easy striking distance of a budget back in the black.

The Ferry Crossing was experiencing a complete makeover, the Stumble Inn now carried an impressive assortment of imported beers to leave sweat stains on brand new tables, haunted home owners filled their rooms with expensive period pieces for added authenticity, and Amanda's family could now enjoy a game of pool anytime they chose in their new club-room basement.

For Mike, money had never been a problem, but now he had enough to launch an academic scholarship fund for the underprivileged, a project he had always of dreamed of starting, should he ever become a man of means. It would seem the only person not to directly benefit from the new industry was its mastermind, Mayor Grey.

Leonard did not mind in the least, for he felt his profit was in the town's success. This new year had all of the promises of progress in the wind, in which he basked to his great satisfaction every time he observed some visible sign of improvement. His biggest victory yet was giving Pamela Holcum a copy of the award notice for a contractor to pave her street in the spring. Miller's Ferry was finally starting to move. It was slow to come out of the gate, but if the next year was anything like the prior, momentum was sure to build, and forward progress was inevitable.

When Leonard pulled his aching truck up to Itchy's Billiard Parlor, he waited while the snowplow made one final pass, clearing out the last of the parking places out front.

Itchy was waiting on the curb outside, ensuring the job was done correctly, and upon its completion, he passed an envelope of cash through the driver's window as payment for his rendered services.

Leonard parked the truck, and as he turned off the ignition, it coughed and sputtered bitterly, until it finally fell silent after a long, desperate gasp. He stepped from the cab to greet Itchy, who was waiting on the sidewalk watching the unfortunate episode. "Morning, Itch. Cold enough for you?"

"Shit, nothing a little antifreeze in the office won't take care of."

"The finest kind."

"How ya' doing, Len, and when do you plan on putting that poor old truck out its misery?"

"Phil's mechanics won't let me. They say they won't let me get rid of her until she makes the million-mile mark. We've been together for some time, and I really don't have any plans of saying goodbye yet."

"Old as she is, I bet there ain't much of her left that's original. I hope you don't plan to leave her out front here for too long. You're liable to scare off my customer base. I swear, guys like you should be made to sign to 'Do Not Resuscitate' agreements when it comes to their vehicles."

"I'm sorry. Were you saying something? I was ignoring you."

"I was just inviting you in for some antifreeze."

The parlor's interior quickly enveloped the two men in its inviting warmth. They hung their coats on ornate brass hooks affixed to the old brick wall near the bandstand and headed back to his office. The barista, one of Itchy's three full-time day employees, took a cue from his boss to mind the store—not that there was much to attend. Very few customers, if any, came in this early. The rest would come shuffling in around lunchtime for gourmet soup and sandwiches.

"Itch, didn't you have five tables the last time I was in here?"

"Sure did. I'm making too much money as a café now. I needed the floor space for more sipping customers. They pay more than the cue stick customers."

"How's the snooker table working out for you?"

"Popular. Ever play it?"

"Not yet. What's it like?"

"A little weird, but the customers like it—somethin' different. Like I said, I don't make much money on the tables no more. Notice there ain't no coin mechanisms? I charge five dollars for balls and unlimited play. Gives folks something to do while they're buying three-dollar coffee drinks."

"You've come a long way, Itchy."

"Thanks. Hey, you should see the new menus. We got a killer cook in the back. I swear, she could make prime rib out of Spam. Come on... you look thirsty."

The two men walked into Itchy's old office, where the last remaining layer of smoke and dust from the old pool hall still resided. Although it retained the character to which Leonard had grown so accustomed, there was a new piece of furniture that startled him by its mere presence.

"New desk, huh, Itch?"

Yeah, for now. I got the old one in the back storage room. Just can't bring myself to get rid of it."

"Then why replace it?"

"Angelina thought it would be more befitting a man of my stature."

"Angelina?"

"Oh, I'm sorry. She's that cook I was tellin' you about. We been seeing each other."

"How's it going?"

"I think we're coming to that stage of the relationship where she tries changing me. She wanted me to get some new kind of prosthetic for my missing arm, said it don't look right with me tucking the jacket arm in my pocket like I do. I went to try one out and didn't like it. I been so used to being lighter on that side that I took to leaning when I strapped it on. Instead, she got me some custom shirts that are sewn where the arm should be. That desk is her latest attempt at change."

"Well... it's very nice."

"It's about as out of place as a whore in a church pew. Look at them carvings and such. She caught me with my feet up on it once and damn near chewed my head clean off. I'll give it a try for a spell, but I think I'll be bringin' the old one back."

"Well, at least she let you keep the old couch," replied Leonard, taking a seat in his usual spot. "I'd hate to have to break in a new one."

"There's some things a woman should just leave alone, and a man's inner sanctum is one of 'em." Itchy produced two cut-crystal glasses and proceeded to pour generous servings of his finest scotch. "A man's office is the very essence of his soul. Could you see Batman's wife trying to cozy up the Batcave with curtains and lace doilies?"

"Batman was married?"

"Well, he could have been, and if'n he had, I bet Mrs. Batman wouldn't be allowed anywhere near his cave. That's the one place in the world where Batman could be himself. Here."

"Thanks. Mmm... oh that's good."

"Should be. That one is old enough to vote." Itchy took his glass around to his desk and sat down in the unfamiliar chair that accompanied it. He proceeded to lean back to place his feet on the edge and then thought better of it, deciding instead to assume a more upright posture, somewhat like a presiding judge. "Guess you heard about ol' Herbert, eh?"

"No. What?" replied Leonard.

"He moved."

"No kidding? Where to?"

"Just over in Circleville. Bragged he was going to be the spearhead of a mass exodus of all that really mattered in this town. Turns out no one wanted to join his wagon train. That poor deluded fool. I almost feel sorry for him."

"Good riddance. We're better off without his kind. If it were up to him, we'd still be teetering at the edge of bankruptcy."

"Can't say I'll miss him. Too much change, I guess. Many of the old timers are still having a tough time with it, but everyone else is just falling right in. I'm even starting to see some of my old customers coming back. I see 'em sneaking bourbon into their coffee drinks, but I still turn a blind eye. Makes for an interesting mix with the Goth clientele. Say, I hear we're getting a couple of new shops up on Main Street."

"Sure are. We're getting a new art gallery/photography studio and an ice cream parlor."

"An art gallery in little ol' Miller's Ferry? No shit?"

"Well it's not really a gallery as you might think, but that sounds better than a picture-framing business."

"Sure, I'll go along with that. I like the new streetlights that are going in."

"They're replicas of Victorian London gas lamps. I think they add a little flair, don't you?"

"Look real pretty. It would seem we are undergoing quite the gentrification. The real question now, is will we be able to sustain it?"

"I've been thinking about that too. This ghost business has been a real shot in the arm for all of us, just what we needed to get going again, but I can't see this going on forever. I guess what I'm looking toward now is the next step. What I'd like to see is a large company or industrial park move in."

"Right, out on Ned Fischer's tract of land. Anything happening with that?"

"I've been going through back channels in the city, trying to stir up business, and things are looking pretty good. The city taxes are making it increasingly difficult for companies to meet their bottom line, so little bedroom communities like this are starting to look like an attractive alternative."

"Yeah, but have you found anyone to bite the hook yet?"

"I have a few nibbles, but I'm still casting. My biggest problem right now is Ned Fischer. He's been talking to someone else about that land."

"That sounds ominous."

"Apparently, someone's been prospecting for a major land grab of his tract, along with several others around his."

"Farming?"

"Nope. I traced it back to a consulting group that usually fronts landfill development companies."

"You're kidding? Not in my back yard."

"Oh, they're just sniffing around for now, but we're going to have to get a move-on before they get serious."

"Good for you, Len. It's reassuring to know there's someone still on watch. Mmm, that is good."

"Say, Itch, you see any of the new residents from town here much?"

"Sure. They seem to like this environment well enough."

"Haven't really met many of them yet."

"It'll take some time before they start settling in. You know, they come out from the city, so in the beginning, that's where they keep their connections. Before you know it, you'll see them popping up in the church congregations, the civic organizations, perhaps even in town government."

"I suppose that's natural. How are the witches doing?"

"The wicked Wiccan girls? They're loads of fun! See 'em here lots, and they're starting to get quite the circle of friends. I don't know if they're kidding or not, but they said they'd be starting up a new coven here in town."

"I hope they're kidding. I don't know if we're ready for that yet."

"Like you said before, this town is a-changing, and we're just going to have change along with it. Remember them gay fellers?"

"Yeah, sure."

"Real nice guys. The one went and designed the kitchen addition I built, free of charge. His partner says he plans to run for school board next election."

"The times really are a-changing. It's a little fast, even for me, but I'm proud of what we've accomplished."

"And you should be. Hell, you've saved us."

"Hold on a sec. It's still too early to call that one."

"For once in your life, would you just shut up and wear the laurels I'm a-tossing at you?"

"Oh, there's no doubt we've come a long way in the last year, but what if sustainability isn't our biggest problem? What if it goes the other way?"

"I don't follow you, Len."

"Suppose Miller's Ferry becomes the kind of place everybody wants to move to? Take, for instance, the gay couple—an engineer and a lawyer, right?"

"Yeah."

"Those two right there have already blown the predominantly blue collar norm. Suppose they are just the beginning of a whole wave of higher-salaried professionals moving into town. Today it's the school board, but how long will it be before they come into positions that could affect our overall cost of living? With higher real estate values and higher property taxes, the citizenry that has roots going back almost 200 years would find themselves living in a town they can't afford anymore. Maybe Herb was right."

"Personally, I think you're getting a little ahead of yourself."

"It's happened before."

"So what are the options, Len? We leave things going the way they were, and the town falls into ruin. You make the town prosper, and we lose our historical families. Then there's the landfill option, and no one will want to live here."

"My money's on the industrial park. Now more than ever, I really think that is the way to go."

"I don't know about you, Mr. Mayor, but I'm kind of excited to see how this thing plays out."

Since Madame Ovary had become a regular guest in Mike's house, Leonard had taken to calling first, in lieu of letting himself in through the kitchen door. Fortunately, she was out of state responding to a possible demonic possession, and Mike was looking forward to Leonard's company.

As he closed the kitchen door behind him, Leonard shook off the cold, along with his overcoat. Mike was already waiting for him with a cold beer.

"Mike, it seems like I haven't seen you in a month of Sundays. How are you?"

"Fine, Len. Fine."

The two took their beers into the living room, which had taken on a slightly disheveled appearance since his last visit—not that it was strewn with junk and trash, just slightly out of its usual, logical order.

"I know. The place is a mess, isn't it?" Mike admitted.

"Compared to my place, it still looks great."

"Still the master of spin, I see. Eunice thinks I'm too uptight and could use a little chaos in my life."

"Relationships are a funny thing. There seems to be a lot of this kind of thing going around these days. Anyway, what have you been up to?"

"Oh, mostly taking it easy. Everything that needs investigating has been done. I help Eunice with her work some. I've been helping displaced spirits find their way over to the other side."

"I see. And what is on the other side?"

"One of the last great mysteries, my friend, and there's only one way to find out."

"She stays pretty busy doing that kind of thing?"

"Sure. For our town, haunted houses have been a booming business, but there are plenty of living folk who could do without the spectral intrusion into their lives."

"Kind of like a pest exterminator, huh?"

"Oh please, Len," Mike answered defensively. "Have you learned nothing from me? These were once people, just like you and me. Most of them don't want to be here anymore than we want them here."

"Alright, alright. I didn't mean to ruffle your feathers. When was your last SI job?"

"Over a month ago."

"You miss it?"

"I'm enjoying the time off, but I am starting to get bored. Amanda is still doing it some. She and her husband have been doing the out-of-town work."

"You're getting some other town involved in this business?"

"Don't worry. We worked out a good no-compete policy. We select the clients and make sure there are no more than one per town. Ever since this became a phenomenon, we had to switch to a phone service so we could handle the increased volume of calls. For customers, we are in want of nothing."

"Why aren't you out there as well?"

"Like I said, I'm enjoying the time off. Besides, her husband is still out of work, and they need the money more than I do."

"That's right… you're quite the philanthropist these days. A scholarship fund, is it?"

"Oh that. Yeah, I'm quite the guy. It's not a big thing, really. It amounts to about $5,000 a year right now. By next year, I want to try to double it."

"Look at you! Just spreading the wealth and sowing the seeds for tomorrow's generation. Good for you, Mike. Good for you."

"So tell me about you and Bea."

"We're still together. She really is a fine woman with a big heart. She keeps hinting at going to that next phase in our relationship, but from where I'm sitting, that could only mean marriage."

"Is that such a bad thing, my friend?"

"You know my track record with wives. The last thing I want to do is screw up a good thing with marriage."

"Since when did you become so cynical? The union between a man and woman can be a beautiful thing. The idea of two like souls sharing their lives until their final days is a warm, comforting notion. If two people fall in love with each other, why shouldn't they get married?"

"Where the hell is this coming from? The last great bachelor espousing the merits of marriage? Why it's... oh, wait a minute! Where is this coming from, Mike?"

Mike tried to break eye contact with his old friend, but felt the gravity of Leonard's piercing stare pulling his attention back.

"You're thinking of marrying Madame Ovary, aren't you?"

"I already bought the ring."

"Ha, ha, ha, ha! You old dog. You made a major life changing-decision without consulting me first?"

"Well, I'm telling you now, aren't I?"

Leonard sat back in the couch, smiling and caressing his chin. "My best friend is getting married. Well, that's just great. Come on and stand up so I can congratulate you properly."

The two old men summoned up the strength to rise from their seats and crossed the short distance to each other. Mike held his hand out to shake, but Leonard brushed it aside and held him in a tight embrace.

"So, who is going to be the best man?" Leonard asked, taking a step back.

"Why would you ask such a question? Just tell me you'll do it."

"I would consider it an honor. When do you plan to officially pop the question?" Leonard asked, sitting back down on the sofa.

"I thought I'd do it this weekend."

"Are you going to do something crazy or just do the bended-knee thing?"

"No, no, nothing like that. If I got down on one knee, I'd need help getting back up. No, I plan to take her to dinner in the city and spring it on her over desert."

"Look at you. You've really grown in this lifetime."

"I'm not the man I was twenty years, and even he was not the man he was twenty years before that. I guess you could say I am a work in progress."

"I'll say. My beer has been sitting on that coffee table this whole time without a coaster."

"And don't think it hasn't been eating me up inside."

"Here," Leonard said, chuckling as he slid a coaster under the offending bottle, "let me set your mind at ease."

"Ahh, a little order has been restored to my universe. It's almost as good as sex."

"You're so easy. This is big, Mike. When do you want to hold the ceremony?"

"Leonard, I haven't even asked her yet."

"I'm sorry. I'm just excited for you... getting married. I hear the words leaving my lips, but they just sound so weird. So I guess there won't be many more nights like this, huh?"

"It would seem I have fallen off the radar as of late, and for that I apologize. Eunice is an amazing woman, and we've really been growing as a couple."

"Don't be sorry, Mike. The fact is, now that the big haunted rush is over, Bea and I have been spending most of our time together. She's really into taking these extension classes down at your last place of employment, and she's been dragging me right along."

"Oh really? What did you take?"

"Modeling clay. I liked it at first, but for the third class, they brought in an adult nude. Never been so uncomfortable in my life." The memory of the youthful man, resplendent in his hair and genitalia, resembling the average Greek god, brought on an involuntary shudder.

"I would have loved to be a fly on the wall for that scene," Mike said, trying to keep a straight face but breaking down in laughter.

"I was fine with woodland animals, but that was more than my sensibilities could stand. We ended up taking pottery in the next room. As it turns out, I'm not half-bad. I made a lovely urn. I intend to one day have my mortal remains interred within that vessel. I think Bea was a little jealous of my progress, so we started taking an Asian cooking class together. She was a natural, of course."

"How did you do?"

"Burned the snow peas in the wok."

"Just look at us. A year ago, would you have ever imagined we'd be sitting here talking about our girlfriends?"

"I guess we never really do stop growing. You're right about not being the man of twenty years ago. I always figured at this point in my life, I'd be set in my ways. I guess I am also a work in progress."

"A great man once said, 'The only constant is change.'"

"He must have had a girlfriend."

"Cheers."

CHAPTER SEVENTEEN

Leonard worked his bowtie unsuccessfully for the third time, ripping it from his neck in disgust.

Beatrice, who sat patiently on the edge of his bed smoothing her dress down for the tenth time in as many minutes, finally stood and took charge of the situation. "I swear, Len, if I leave it up to you, we'll never make it to your best friend's wedding. Why didn't you get a clip-on?" she asked, walking over to him where he stood in front of the bureau mirror.

"Philistine, be gone with you!" he replied in irritation. "I have never and will never succumb to so barbarous a convenience. It is a lazy man's contrivance and will find no place in my wardrobe," he ranted while looking into the mirror, refusing to acknowledge her advance.

"Stand still, you old fool, and let me do it." She stood behind him, looking over his shoulder, and yanked the bowtie out of his hand.

"I know how to do it. I'm just nervous, that's all."

"Don't be silly, dear. Of course I know you can do it. Now let's see… over here, under there, fold that, loop around through, and tuck. There. Not bad for an old broad, huh?"

"Not bad at all," he replied, inspecting her work in the mirror. "Where did you learn to do that?"

"I took a class."

"Of course. Thank you, Bea," he replied, turning around in her still outstretched arms and hugging her around her waist. He smiled and kissed her softly. "I'm a lucky man to have you."

"Well, someone has to keep you on time. Now let's go."

Unwilling to be seen in Leonard's old truck, Bea insisted he drive her Plymouth. Although it lacked some of the luster that once gleamed on its speckles exterior, it was clean and reliable. After buckling in, they drove off together to a wedding that had already assembled. The fortunate thing about living in a small town was that one never had to travel far when running late.

Mike, who subscribed to no organized religion, insisted upon a wedding at the park in the center of town. The ceremony had been booked for the second weekend in May, and fortune smiled on the man and his bride in the way of a cloudless blue sky and a soft warm breeze.

Mike was pacing nervously as Leonard and Bea drove into the crowded parking lot. "Leonard!" he called out, advancing on the car. "Must you drag your sorry ass on this of all days? Oh, hello, Bea."

"Hi, Mike. Sorry. It was all his fault."

"Afraid the bride will get cold feet?" asked Leonard as he climbed out of the car.

"Well, come on. We've waited long enough," replied Mike, hastening his friend away and leaving Bea alone to find her own way.

The old professor hustled Leonard down the aisle, which was defined by folding chairs, up into the gazebo, and to the man who would be officiating the ceremony. Although Eunice left all the details up to Mike, she made one modest request where the ceremony was concerned. Although Mike had recently become a born-again agnostic, his desire was for a Justice of the Peace to join them together. However, Eunice insisted there be at least some level of spirituality about the event, so after much arguing with her betrothed, they settled on a former Buddhist who had only recently been ordained as a Methodist minister. They both agreed he had something to offer everyone.

Once the groom, his best man, and the maid of honor were all in their respective places, the minister nodded his assent for Angelina, the organist, to commence with the "Wedding March." As the first few notes echoed across the park, a temporary blue tarpaulin was pulled aside at the Rotary Club picnic pavilion to reveal the bride and her escort, Itchy Jackson, who commenced with their relaxed stroll to the gazebo.

"Isn't she a vision?" whispered Mike in Leonard's ear.

"She looks beautiful. Her dress is very... uh, well, colorful."

"She's a practical woman. She didn't want to buy a dress she could only wear once. It does have a bit of a gypsy flair, doesn't it?"

"All that's missing is a crystal ball."

"Why does Itchy look different to me?"

"Because he has two arms today."

"Well I'll be! He sure does! The prosthetic looks very natural."

"He hates it, but he puts it on for special occasions."

"I can't thank him enough for doing this."

"He told me it comes as part of package deal when you hired Angelina to cater the reception."

Eunice and Itchy ascended the three steps into the gazebo and joined the rest of the wedding party. Eunice was so giddy over the event that when she broke away from Itchy to stand by Mike's side, she forgot his arm was artificially bent at the elbow. As she stepped away with her arm still interlocked in his, it produced an audible click at the shoulder as he turned to walk away, forcing the prosthetic limb behind his torso into an unnatural dangle. The few guests in the congregation who were not familiar with Itchy gasped at the perceived dislocation and puzzled when he effortlessly snapped it back into place without so much as a wince. Once all the mechanical joints were properly aligned, he straightened it out to hang naturally by his side.

"Friends," the minister started, "we are gathered together here in the sight of God and in the presence of these witnesses to join together Michael and Eunice in a strictly non-denominational, yet conventional marriage. The covenant of marriage was established by God and sanctified by Jesus Christ, as He graced a wedding in Cana of Galilee. It is, therefore, not to be entered into unadvisedly, but reverently, discreetly, and in the love of God—or, in Michael's case, to that higher order to which he chooses to subscribe—"

"That's okay, Reverend. You can say God for me too," interrupted Mike with a reassuring nod.

Eunice beamed, and Leonard smiled with a raised eyebrow at his friend.

"Very well… That into this holy estate these two come now to be joined."

At this point, many of the older ladies in the congregation began to pat the corner of their eyes with tissues. Attracted by the spectacle of the ceremony, curious onlookers began to gather at the periphery of the park.

"Michael and Eunice, I require and charge you both, as you stand in the presence of God, before whom the secrets of all hearts are disclosed, that having duly considered the holy covenant you are about to make, you do now declare before these people your pledge of faith, each to the other. Who presents Eunice to be married to Michael?"

"I do yer Honor… uh, yer Holiness," replied Itchy, raising his working arm. Itchy gave Mike a reassuring pat on his back and took a seat in the front row with the congregation.

"Ladies and gentlemen, Michael and Eunice have elected to exchange their own vows."

The bride and groom turned to each other and joined hands.

Mike cleared his throat, and began his pledge. "My dearest Eunice, in the time we have been together, I find you are the reason behind all I do in my life. It is for you I wake each day, and it is for you I rest. It is for you I laugh, and for you I cry. It is for you I want to become the man I was meant to be. My darling Eunice, I pledge my unwavering love to you, and only you, through the bright days to come and the dark times we have yet to face together. I pledge to lift you when you are down and celebrate every day we have together as if it were the first. I vow to keep these promises throughout the life I have left on this Earth."

The gentle pats at eyes were now widespread throughout the congregation, with copious amounts of tissues passed amongst the guests.

Eunice was stunned by her groom's words, and struggled to regain her composure. "Mike, this is my first time at marriage, so you'll have to bear with me if I make mistakes. But that aside, I promise to love you until I cross over. I promise to never nag you, or complain about you, or try to make you into a man you were not meant to be. I will treasure your soul here and in the hereafter, which, coming from anyone else, might not mean that much. I promise to devote the rest of my life to being your loving wife in good times and in bad. Most importantly, I will never say you can't spend time with your friend Leonard, when you two want to drink beer and figure out the mysteries of the universe."

"She's a keeper," whispered Leonard in his friend's ear.

"May I have the rings?" the minister asked. "These rings are an outward and visible sign of an inward and spiritual grace, signifying to us the union between Jesus Christ and his church and to all the uniting of Michael and Eunice in holy marriage. Bless, Oh Lord, the giving of these rings that they who wear them may abide in your peace and continue in your favor all the days of their lives, through Jesus Christ our Lord. Amen."

Mike and Eunice accepted the rings and placed them on each other's fingers, while exchanging their final vows.

"You have declared your consent and your vows before God and this congregation. May God confirm your covenant and fill you both with grace. Now that Michael and Eunice have given themselves to one another and have declared the same by the joining of hands and the giving and receiving of rings, I pronounce they are husband and wife together, in the name of the Father, the Son, and the Holy Spirit. You may now kiss the bride."

With that, Mike took Madame Ovary in a full embrace and placed upon her lips a kiss that evoked joyous applause from the congregation of this world and the next.

"Itchy, you and Angelina have outdone yourselves," said Leonard, biting into another hors d'oeuvre.

"Oh hell, Mr. Mayor, it's just one more facet of this diamond in the rough."

"No really, you fixed the place up great, and who'd have thunk of using the pool tables to serve food?"

"Originally, I was just concerned with people spilling stuff on the felt, but with a sheet of plywood and some table linens, I found form and function."

"I love the ice sculpture."

"It's plastic. Every so often, Angelina secretly spritzes it with water to make it look like it's dripping."

"Really? Get out."

"Honest Injun."

"Where'd you get the band?"

"They're something of a house band now. When they ain't too stoned, they make it in here most weekends to play."

"It sure was nice of them to let Belt Buckle Bob sing."

"He sings in here quite a bit when the karaoke feller ain't up at the Stumble Inn. You might say he's become something of a regular. It's in his honor that I now serve genuine Cowboy Coffee. I cook it in an old, baked enamel coffee pot I picked up at the Salvation Army. Of course, he's the only one what drinks it."

"Look at Mike and Eunice out there," said Leonard, looking out at the sole couple on the dance floor.

"Yeah. They make fine couple, don't they?"

"She's quite a woman."

"And that's quite a woman you got in Bea. Since hooking up with you, she's really come out of her armor-plated shell."

"Oh, she was never that bad."

"You know how you always come in here and sing 'There's trouble right here in River City?'"

"Sure."

"Well, she used to be part of a quiet coalition that thunk it."

"Really? Bea?"

"You're my friend and all, and I would never say anything to change your opinion of her, so you must know I would never lie. There was a time when that woman did not like me one bit, but I guess since I turned the place around, and then she started hooking up with you, she's taken the time to give me a kind word or two. She even gave me a free history of the old place, just in case I ever want to get it checked for spooks."

"She really is a brand new woman, Itch, and I must confess I've fallen pretty hard for her."

"Any plans of gettin' hitched yerself?"

"Why does love have to equal marriage? I really like this one, and I am in no rush to make her my third ex."

"Slow down there, Len. No need to bite my head off. Just seemed like a natural question to ask after Mike getting married and all."

"Oh, I'm sorry, Itch. I guess it has become a touchy subject with me."

"Why? Has Bea been after you?"

"No, nothing like that. If I asked, I'm pretty sure she'd say yes, but she's never even brought it up."

"Maybe that's the problem. Her talkin' marriage might just validate any secret notions you've had on the matter."

"You know what your problem is, Itch? You think too much."

"Looks like I hit a nerve. Well, for what it's worth, I been thinkin' of asking Angelina myself."

"No way! You?"

"'These time, they are a-changin.' You know, after a while, being alone kinda gets old."

"My congratulations to you then, Itch."

"Oh I didn't say I was going to ask her, but I have been turning the idea around in my brain some. If'n I do, I want you to be my best man."

"I'm honored, and I would be honored to be your best man as well."

"Thank you, Mr. Mayor. I'll get back to you on that issue. Now, there's something else I've been wanting to talk to you about. Have you been keeping up with Ned Fischer at all?"

"Not really. Why?"

"I think that's one relationship you need to rekindle, and quick. You know the gay couple I've been talking about?"

"Sure the lawyer and the—"

"Yep. The lawyer is the one who's keeping me informed of certain events at the county building. Turns out there has already been a land grab around Ned's property, and it ain't a farmer what's doing it."

"I've heard nothing on the landfill issue."

"And I doubt you will until it's too late. Like I said, you gotta act quick."

"No one has even discussed zoning yet. Officially, no one has even used the word 'landfill' that I've heard."

"Don't mean it won't happen. It seems to me, a man wouldn't be buying up land unless he knew he had the adjoining parcel in his back pocket. The laws on eminent domain and zoning arbitration are all kind of murky, given where the location is in regards to the village. Unless Ned's parcel is being put to some other use before they tip their hand, you might just find we have no choice in the matter."

"They wouldn't dare."

"Been out that way lately? There are surveyors' stakes all over the place."

"That's not a good sign. Sounds like I need to pay our farmer friend a little visit. In the mean time, you'll have to excuse me while I make my toast. You know… always a best man, never a groom."

Chapter eighteen

The driveway to Ned Fischer's house was long and rutted, with many deep potholes, much to the dismay of Leonard's truck. At its conclusion was a simple white clapboard house with dull, peeling paint and shutters that sagged under the influence of decades of weather and gravity. Ned was out front under the hood of his own truck when Leonard arrived. As he parked, Ned pulled his head out and looked curiously over at the truck that coughed and sputtered its way into silence. Leonard climbed out of the cab and strolled around to Ned, as if this were some chance encounter. "Morning, Ned. Time for a little wrench turning, I see."

"I never thought I'd see a truck in worse shape than mine, but you win that prize. Good morning, Len. How are you?" he said, wiping the grease from his hands so he could give a proper shake.

"Oh, fair to middlin'. And you?"

"No worse for the wear, I guess. What brings you out this way?"

"Can't a fella just be social?"

"I know why you're here, so let's just skip it."

"Alright, Ned. I'm here about the landfill deal. Have you sold yet?"

"Told 'em I'd sleep on it, but with what they've offered me, I'm kept up most nights."

"I see. You know how everyone else would feel about this, Ned."

"Can't say I care much. The kids have all grown and moved out into their own lives, so I have nobody to leave the farm. The missus and I have become pretty partial to warm weather as of late, so whatever they do on my land, I don't reckon I'll be able to see it from my next house in Florida."

"Florida? What do you want to go there for? You'll have to learn Spanish."

"We'll manage."

"For God's sake, Ned, look at what you'd be leaving behind—just a big, stinking heap of trash. Is that the way you want to be remembered? You have roots in this community. Your ancestors were some of its earliest settlers. I know this, because I've had coffee at your kitchen table, right under the framed copy of the original deed. In town, we're your neighbors, your friends, your family. I just want you to think on that for while."

"Pretty speech, Mr. Mayor, but I can't pay my bills with that. I've been struggling damn near my whole life to keep my head above water, and suddenly the lottery is in town and wants to pay me big."

"How big?"

"Oh, just a measly $850,000 big."

"Phew! That is a big number. You could buy a lot of sunshine with that much."

"It's a lot more than the $400,000 your realtor thinks it's worth."

"But that's not such a bad number either, is it? When we first talked, you thought it was a great number."

"It suddenly got a whole lot smaller."

"There has to be something we can do here, Ned. What would it take to make you change your mind on this? Please... I'm begging."

"Match it, and it's yours."

"Hell, Ned, you might as well be asking for eight million in this economy. No one will pay that to put an industrial park here."

"Not my problem, Len."

"We'll get an injunction on the zoning."

"Good luck with that one. This is just past your particular zone of influence, Len. Look, I'm not trying to be the bad guy here, but this is my retirement we're talkin' about. I'll give you one month. After that, you're on your own."

For the first time in his mayoral career, Leonard found his back was to the wall. As dire as things had seemed in the past, this time there was a deadline, and the clock didn't have many ticks or tocks left. He was angry at himself for not keeping a more involved relationship with Ned Fischer, for while he rested on the laurels of his recent successes, he never saw the land grab until it was too late. Moreover, he was disappointed with Ned. His family had lived many generations in the area, and the thought of Ned being so eager to sell out as quickly as he was about to, chafed at Leonard badly. If only he could honor his end with a financial match, there was still hope, slim as it was.

Leonard jumped out of his truck and bounded up to his floor in the administration building in town, bursting into Lori's office. Out of breath, he fished through his briefcase for a thick folder of papers.

"Good morning, Len. There are—"

"Not now, Lori. We have a situation, and I've got no time to bring you up to speed. Here," he said, putting the folder on her desk. "Everything you need to know is in this folder. You need to go through it, understand it, and get me on the calendars this week of everyone involved."

"Okay, but there are—"

Leonard breezed past her desk, cutting her off mid-sentence, and opened the door to his office. Seated around his desk were four ladies ranging in age from sixty to eighty, their hands folded in their laps or clutching their purses. They all turned their heads in unison upon his surprise entrance.

"Good morning, ladies. Will you excuse me just one minute?" He closed the door gently behind and walked back to Lori's desk. "Who are those ladies, and why are they are here?"

"I tried to tell you. They're here to talk to you about the alternative zoning."

"Yeah, but what do they want?"

"They call themselves a 'cross section of the disenfranchised faithful Christians'. They feel our mortal souls are in danger with all of the ghost business going on in this town, and they want to put a stop to it."

"But I don't recognize any of them. Are they even from this town?"

"I don't know, Len. You'll have to talk to them."

Leonard walked back into his office, met by the disapproving gaze of his newfound critics. He put his case down on the floor next to his desk, sat down, and removed a legal pad and pen from his drawer. "Now, how can I help you?"

"We're here to put a stop to what you're doing in Miller's Ferry, Mayor Grey," replied the youngest of the group, seated to his far left.

"I see. Before we start, would you mind introducing yourselves please?"

"Certainly. My name is Alma Young, this is Jillian Grey—no relation, I'm sure—next to her is Martha Schlemer, and on the end is Gloria Lister. We're here to put a stop to your unholy activities in this town."

"Sure, but one moment. Mrs. Schlemer, are you, by chance, related to Herbert Schlemmer?"

"I am his mother," the oldest of the coalition replied.

"Ah, I think I'm seeing more clearly now. He just moved to Circleville, right?"

"That is correct. Although I should be happy he would move so close to me, he only came because you ran him out of town."

"Mrs. Schlemer, I assure you I did not run your son or anyone else out of town."

"Oh yes you did. You turned this perfectly wonderful town into a den of demon-worshipping homosexuals. He told me all about it."

"Mr. Mayor," interrupted Alma Young, "I think I should start by saying none of us are from Miller's Ferry. With the exception of Martha, the rest of us have only distant relations here at best."

"Then why the sudden interest in us?"

"We certainly do not condone what you have been doing here, and we can only imagine what kind of spell you must have put on everyone to go along with this evil. The fact is, what you are doing in this town is now stirring interest in other towns, including ours. Already, your ghost people have been snooping around in houses in our neighborhoods, and we will not let you undermine our Christian values."

"This whole thing is an abomination against God!" declared Martha.

"First of all, I have never cast any spells in my entire life. I'm a Methodist."

The ladies all began rolling their eyes and clucking their tongues. Under the breath of one, he could have sworn he heard the words "It figures."

"Ladies, I assure you this is a good town, with good family values."

"Sure, if you're the Addams family," snapped Gloria.

"The homeowners in our town have individual rights to commune with anyone they choose, even if that is a ghost. These 'haunted houses' have always been as such, and our homeowners have elected to share them with the rest of world."

"The only reason you have ghosts in your houses is because you made a pact with Satan!" yelled Martha. "I know, because my son told me so."

"Herbert told you that?" asked Leonard. "That is a horrible thing to say. I go to church every Sunday, and I can tell you I am a God-fearing man."

"You should be afraid of God, you...you Methodist! It's going to take a lot more than a covered dish to get back in his good graces," cautioned Alma.

The rest nodded their heads in full agreement.

Leonard sat back in his chair and sighed, looking at each of the ladies in turn. "Again, I want to know what you want from me. The tourism we have created here is not going to stop, even if I wanted it to, which I don't."

"Mr. Mayor, we represent a large, motivated army of concerned citizens from each of our respective towns. We are working within our own town governments to stop any momentum in duplicating your dark plan, but that is not enough. You have been the example of how to turn a town to the devil, and so you shall be made an example of to all the other towns when you anger the church."

"What did you have in mind, Alma?"

"That's 'Mrs. Young' to you! We know your tourist season is starting back up again, and we plan to make a strong showing when it does. We will join all of our forces and do everything within our power to disrupt your little show so everyone else will see what waits for them if they follow your lead. Come on, ladies. We're finished here."

The four stood and headed for the door in single file, Alma Young bringing up the rear.

As she left the office, she paused and turned back to Leonard. "The judgment of God is coming swift and sure, Mr. Mayor. You have been warned."

Leonard stacked this crisis atop his others and sighed deeply. All he ever wanted in this job was to be the guy everybody liked. It was never part of his career plan to be a crusader and/or a villain. All of a sudden, the prospect of running away to Florida with Ned Fischer and his wife looked very appealing.

"Wow!" said Lori, bursting into his office with a cup of coffee. "I heard the whole thing. Do you think they're anything of a threat?" she asked, handing him the cup.

Leonard didn't answer. He reached into his bottom drawer and pulled out a bottle of bourbon, from which he poured a generous shot into his coffee cup. He finished christening his palate with a heavy slug directly from the bottle and then put it back into its drawer.

"Wow again. It's a little early, don't you think?"

"Did you read the file?"

"Something about Ned Fisher's land being used for an industrial park? Sounds like a good move."

"There's a development company looking to plant a landfill there instead, and they just made Ned an offer he can't refuse."

"A landfill? I haven't heard anything about this."

"Nor will you, until it's too late."

"So it's a done deal?" she said, sitting in one of the empty seats.

"He'll proffer the deal for an industrial park if we can find a matching offer."

"Well, that's good news. So those people you want me to call and schedule, those are rival developers?"

"Correct, but the number is $850,000, and he's only giving us one month to make it happen."

The gravity of Leonard's statement settled into Lori. "There's no way."

"I'm grabbing at straws here, but there's plenty enough land there to be further subdivided into residential as well."

"The real estate market has been soft, Len. It would take a miracle to pull something like that off in just one month. Can't Ned give us a little more time?"

"He already has a house picked out in Florida and wants to retire there before too long. He was pretty adamant about wrapping up all of this in the next thirty days."

"If that landfill goes in, our real estate values will plummet. Everything we've worked so hard for will be for nothing."

"That's just the beginning. I heard a rumor from a friend of mine downtown. Based on this change of events, the city of Cincinnati is looking at putting in tracts of Section Eight housing on the excess land those developers have been gobbling up. We barely have the infrastructure in place to accommodate what modest growth I have planned, but this? The school will overflow with new kids, so we'll have to bring in trailers. Taxes will go up to meet the cost of improvements, and it only keeps getting worse."

"Oh, Ned, what have you done? Do you have another cup back there? I could use a shot—or three."

CHAPTER NINETEEN

Itchy was staring down the length of an upheld pool cue when Leonard rushed into the parlor. As soon as Itchy saw him, he put the stick down and motioned for Leonard to follow him back into the office. Itchy closed the door and immediately took a seat behind his new desk. "I'd offer you a drink, but something tells me you want to talk business."

"Thanks, Itch. You're right, I'm not going on a bender, I just need to think, and you're my best sounding board. I guess bad news travels fast?"

"Yep, and this is about as bad as it gets. What kind of options we looking at?"

"A lot of maybes, but nothing solid yet."

"Tell me."

"I've found one company so far that is a definite for the industrial park. They plan to do late-model car conversions to hybrid and/or electric, with their own line of electric cars to come out in two years."

"Neat."

"Another company wants to set up a shop for after-market Caterpillar parts, and another plans to open a large machine shop."

"How many do you need to fill the park?"

"Seven, with a couple of new neighborhoods to be built right next door. If I only had more time, I might be able to swing it, but there's another hitch. No one will sign unless all of the site development has been done first."

"Oh. That ain't cheap."

"You ain't kidding. I'm hoping I can get a developer to buy the land and recoup the cost through sale or lease, but I still don't think we'll be able to get anywhere near Ned's price with only three businesses going in."

"Make that five."

"Huh?"

"Remember the gay guys?"

"Oh please, Itchy. We've talked about them plenty as the 'gay guys.' Why don't you give them names?"

"Ha, I guess you're right. They're a real nice couple of fellas. Eddie—he's the lawyer—has been trying to talk his partner James into opening up his own engineering firm for years. Turns out they're both loaded, and James wants to set up shop over in the park. He's ready, with a staff of thirty-five to boot."

"That's great. Who's the other?"

"One of the wicked Wiccan girls, Melanie. She is the general manager of a small plastic injection mold company in the city. She has them talked into opening up a new, larger facility in the park. Eventually, they'll close their doors in the city and move all of their operations out here."

"Itchy, you never fail to amaze me. My God, man! Two more, and we may just be able to pull this off."

"Still a lot to do in only one month."

"Twenty-five days now."

"How're things looking in town?"

"Ready for the haunted season to open tonight."

"Heard you had some protestors up in your office on Monday."

"You'll never guess who one of them was—Herbert's mother."

"Why, that bitter asshole, sending his own mom into his fight! I have no respect for him now. I gather they don't like the whole ghost thing?"

"Nope. They called us a bunch of 'demon-worshiping homosexuals.' I'd love to hear how Eddie and James would respond to that one. That old woman better watch out when she tangles with a lawyer. Like I said, he's loaded, and you don't get that way being a sorry attorney."

"Yeah, Itchy, this is going to be one interesting month. Lawyers and Wiccans and landfills… oh my."

It had been about as stressful a week for Leonard as it could get. The strains of leadership in the small community had taken a serious toll, and it now affected him on a more personal level.

"Come on, Len. It happens to a lot of guys," said Bea, leaning on one elbow in the bed next to a very somber mayor, who was staring up at the ceiling.

"The words every man wants to hear."

"As old as your pipes are, it was bound to happen sooner or later."

"You're not doing much for my morale, Bea."

"When did you take your, um, vitamin?"

"Is that what we're calling it now?"

"Sounds better than the V word."

"About a half hour ago."

"How long does it take to work on you?"

"Not sure. It should be kicking in soon."

"You want to talk about it?"

"Not especially."

"Do you want me to do that thing?"

"What thing?"

"You know…" she replied, slowly circling a finger on his chest.

"Oh, that thing. Sure. It couldn't hurt."

Bea pulled the bed covers back and prepared to perform 'the thing' when a subtle purring from the pocket of Leonard's pants draped over a chair arm intruded upon their moment.

"Damn… and I think I'm almost there. Hold on a second."

"Just let it go to voicemail."

"This will only take a moment." Leonard got out of the bed, and fished his vibrating cell phone from his pants. "Hello… What?… WHAT?… Oh, for crying out loud!… Sure, sure. I'll be there." Leonard proceeded to pull his clothes together and get dressed. "I'm sorry, sweetheart, but I have to run."

"But I was going to do—"

"The thing, I know. Can you put that pot on simmer until I get back? I have an emergency."

"Sure. I'll watch a little TV while I'm waiting. Now you get back here soon, I don't know how long this pot is going to simmer. Where are you off to?"

"The Hofflers' house. There has been an incident."

The street outside of the Hofflers' house had two of the five village squad cars parked at queer angles to the sidewalk, as if they had just arrived at the scene of the crime of the century. Their blue lights illuminated the neighborhood in dazzling blue and red, playing off the walls of nearby houses. The Hofflers were outside the front door, surrounded by three police officers, Ernie was giving his statement, and Robert was handcuffed.

Leonard parked his truck next to one of the squad cars and charged up the front walk to the crowded front stoop. "Billy, why is that man handcuffed?" demanded Leonard of the oldest officer, a young man of twenty-seven.

"He's being arrested for assault with a deadly weapon, Mr. Mayor."

"What? This is insane. Look at the man! He's in his eighties. For crying out loud, take those cuffs off of him now."

"But, sir, it's procedure in a crime of this type."

"Do you really want me to call the chief? Look, I'll take full responsibility for whatever happens."

Billy stared at the ground for the requisite ten seconds it required to make it look as if he were actually considering it, and then made a good show of reluctantly removing the cuffs from Robert's wrists while shaking his head in disbelief.

"Now, what is this all about?"

"Well, sir—" started Billy.

"I'll tell you what it is," yelled Ernie, cutting the young officer off. "We were provoked by that woman there," he continued, pointing at the senior citizen sitting on the stoop, holding her head.

"Alma?" said Leonard.

"I want that man arrested, and I mean now. He hit me!" she replied, pointing at Robert.

"And you're crazy, you old cow. Just who the hell do you think you are?" replied Robert, showing obvious trouble in retaining his spittle or his dentures.

"What happened, Ernie?"

"It's opening night, and we're one of the more popular houses now. We had a fair amount of people showing up to take tours, when this one shows up with a guided group from the park. Right when I'm in the middle of my spiel, she whips out a Bible and starts yelling 'I cast you out, unclean spirit' and a bunch of other stuff."

"That's from The Excorcist," added Alma, by way of explanation. "That's where I learned to perform exorcisms."

"I see," replied Leonard. "Go on, Ernie."

"Well, she was going nuts, walking around pointing her finger at the tourists and yelling at them, telling them they are all going to hell. So Robert, hearing what was going on from the living room, comes out into the hallway. Out of nowhere, she runs up and slaps his head with her Bible and goes on with her exorcism again. She nearly knocked him off his feet with that big ol' book of hers!"

"I was defending myself. I don't know who this crazy woman is. I was in fear for my life, so I fought her off with my cane."

"Aren't those the magic words, Officer?" asked Leonard.

"I'm no lawyer," said Billy, "but I think it's a pretty good defense."

"Perhaps a little back story on this would help. Alma here, along with three of her friends, walked into my office and threatened to disrupt our tourism. I thought it would just be some good old-fashioned 'right of assembly,' but now I see they have different plans in mind. She attacked that man."

"I know my rights!" screamed Alma. "I was exercising my freedom to exorcise."

"Ma'am, you're going to be hard pressed to find that one in any law book," replied the young officer.

"I answer to the law of God!"

"That may be, ma'am, but for tonight, I'm going to have to take you in and sort this all out in the morning."

With the threat of jail suddenly looming over her head, Alma lost all of her steam and went back to pitifully cradling the lump on her head, trying to evoke whatever sympathy might be available.

"Officer," said Leonard, "perhaps as a gesture of goodwill and as a personal favor to me, you might consider escorting Alma and her group out of town instead of to the jailhouse?"

Alma looked up at the conversation.

"So what's it going to be, Alma? Jail or home tonight?"

Now Alma stared up for her requisite ten seconds and mumbled in defeated fashion, "Home."

"How many of your group are here tonight, ma'am?" asked Billy, but Alma remained tight-lipped.

"It's just the four of you, isn't it?" said Leonard.

She replied with a saddened nod of her head.

"Not much of an army, huh? Billy, why don't you let her stew in the back of your squad car while we find the others."

"Never mind that," interrupted Alma, digging her cell phone out of her purse. "I'll text them to meet me back at the car," she continued, busily pushing buttons on her phone.

"Billy, why don't you take her to her car and give these ladies the escort we discussed."

After completing her signal to retreat to the other ladies, Alma returned her phone to her purse. As she readied herself for standing up, her eyes fell on the mayor's waist. "Ahhh!" she shrieked, pointing at Leonard's swollen groin, which had finally responded to his so-called vitamin. "He's possessed! Where's my Bible?"

"Do you have something in your pocket, Mr. Mayor, or are you just happy to see us?" chuckled Ernie with a knowing wink, obviously a member of the secret vitamin club.

"Well, that didn't take long, sweetie. Everything alright?" asked Beatrice.

"Yes… and no. We'll talk about it tomorrow," replied Leonard, taking off his shirt and unfastening his belt. "Are you still simmering?"

"I'm good and hot. Now where were we? Oh yes, I was going to do that thing to you."

"No time for the thing, Bea. We need to get right to it."

"Not much on foreplay, are you? Goodness," she exclaimed as Leonard took off the last of his garments. "He's back."

"And he's ready."

Chapter twenty

Leonard and Mike walked into the Ferry Landing amidst the mid-breakfast crowd. As soon as people looked up from their plates to see who had entered the restaurant, the sideways glances and snickering whispers began. Leonard tried to meet these looks with a stern glare but was only met with more smiles and giggles.

"What's wrong with everyone, Len? Do I have a booger or something?" asked Mike, turning away from the attention.

"Never mind them, Mike. Silly people engaging in sillier gossip. Come on."

Leonard led Mike through the restaurant with as much dignity as he could muster, but found a similar response upon his entrance in the next dining room. He breezed past the tables to the one that basked in the early morning sun, avoiding any potential eye contact. Everyone at the table seemed unfamiliar to him, as they contorted their faces and tried to look away in an effort to avoid breaking out into laughter. Beatrice sat as upright and proper as she could in the face of the humiliation that she now shared.

"Good morning, everybody," said Leonard in an attempt to call the group to order. "I'm sure you all know Professor Mike Pennington. I invited him to join us today."

Happy to break away from the awkwardness Leonard's presence had evoked, they all cheerily welcomed Mike to breakfast.

Leonard motioned to the waitress to bring two menus, and turned his attention to the table. "Well let's get down to it. By now, you should all be up to speed on what is developing over at Ned Fischer's place."

Slowly, heads around the table nodded in confirmation of his statement, but eyes were still averted to avoid the inevitable response to looking directly at him.

"I don't think I need to stress the severity of this situation. If the landfill deal goes through, we'll be looking at some hard times ahead, and I mean hard."

It started a little at first, as Leonard's last word still hung in the air. Jenny chirped and tried to cover her mouth that spread outwards into a huge grin. Jerald tried biting his lip, to no avail. The Drescher Four really got it going by breaking out into loud guffaws, which resulted in the same response from everybody else except Leonard, Bea, and Mike.

"I don't understand, Len. Why is everybody laughing?" asked Mike aloud.

"We're laughing at the mayor's boner!" yelled Robert Hoffler between chuckles.

This last announcement echoed throughout the restaurant, which sent everyone at every table into hysterics.

"Oh, for crying out loud!" huffed Leonard.

Beatrice still maintained her focus on the plate in front of her out of respect for Leonard but soon started snickering herself.

"Fine!" shouted Leonard, standing up to address the entire restaurant. "Let's get it all out. The mayor had a boner last night. Come on and laugh it up so we can return to some semblance of normalcy."

"I think I've been missing out on something by not coming to breakfast, Len. Do you always share that kind of information with the general public?" asked Mike, still trying to figure out what was going on.

Eventually the laughter died down, and the group as a whole did, in fact, return to some sense of normalcy, with the exception of few errant giggles.

"Back to business. The rumor mill runs pretty swiftly in this town, but I think it's time to bring in the press on the landfill issue. Tom, can you handle that?"

"Sure, Len. You are right about the rumor mill. It has been very Viagrous," he said, which brought about a second round of laughter at the table. "I'm sorry, Len, but this is just too good," he continued, wiping away the tears that had formed in his eyes. "I'm sorry. I'll stop. Sure, we'll prepare a statement and get it to the local press."

"Good. Maybe the court of public opinion will have more sway on this matter by the time it gets to the county courthouse. Listen, I do not want there to be any reprisal on Ned, so hold back his name. Also, I want you to really stress the importance of this industrial park. Ned is still willing to work with us, so if there is any chance of striking a deal with him, I don't want anything to screw this up with bad blood. Onto other things... Jerald, how is your son doing these days?"

"Oh, he's fine, Mr. Mayor."

Leonard waited for something substantive but received only a friendly smile. "I mean with the real estate office."

"Oh, sure, sure. Things have been going gangbuster, you betcha. There is now, for the first time in our town history, a waiting list to buy anything in the Historic District, with a premium on houses with the alternative zoning. What's interesting is that he's been doing a fair amount of sales in the developments as well. All in all, it's a real seller's market."

"That's great, Jerald."

"I understand you're looking to subdivide the areas surrounding the industrial park?"

"It's still too early for that, but one should beget the other. Bea," Leonard continued, turning his attention to his still-blushing girlfriend seated next to him, "what was the head count for the park tours this weekend?"

Bea finished chewing and swallowing her pancakes and then put her fork down gently onto her plate. "Only 1,000, but the season just started."

"Tom, where do we stand on advertisement?"

"Our tri-folds are now at every interstate rest stop in Ohio."

"Good, but I think we need to be more ambitious. See if you can put together a calendar of events for this year and get it up on the website. Speaking of which, I think we need to work on its appearance. Also, let's start looking into television advertisements. I know there isn't a lot in the budget for that, but we could probably find some good deals on late-night timeslots, perhaps public access channels. Mike, how are things with SI?"

"Oh, it's my turn. I'm starting to get business again, or I should say a different kind of business. I've had three new requests—or at least Eunice has—to rid houses of more unwanted ghosts."

"Let me get this straight," said Robert Hoffler, leaning in closer to the table. "They want you to perform… an exorcism?"

"You'll have to excuse him, Professor," interrupted his brother Ernie. "We had an incident this weekend, and now it's all he can think about."

"Maybe that crazy woman was right, Ernie," replied Bob. "Maybe we need to be concerned about our mortal souls."

"Oh rubbish, Bob. Try to forget about it. I'm sorry, Professor. You were saying?"

"Yes, well, Eunice is not really an exorcist. She just helps lost souls find their way to other side."

"What other side?" snapped Robert.

"We're on this side, which isn't the other side. The other side of here."

Robert looked at Mike, adjusting his loose dentures with his tongue while waiting for some kind of epiphany. "What the hell does that mean?"

"If you feel more comfortable with the idea of heaven, we'll call it that. To be honest, even Eunice doesn't really know what the other side is all about; only that most spirits want to go there."

"I think what everybody fails to see here," interrupted Leonard, "is that this is a reversing trend. We've had a few people ask the professor and Eunice to rid houses already, but they were mostly houses without any zoning. I thought we were past all that."

"Oh, Len, I don't think we can call it a trend yet. It's only three."

"Do any of them have zoning?"

"Uh, all of them do."

The table all looked to each other with grave looks as they started coming to the same conclusions.

"Like he said, it's only three," said Leonard. "Just in case, Tom, I only want you to get estimates on those television slots. We'll see how this pans out before we commit to anything. Jenny, it's been a hell of a tax year, hasn't it?"

"Yes," she replied shyly. "I talked to the city manager last week, and we're looking at making a lot of improvements this summer. New roads in town, and now we're looking at extending municipal water and sewer out into the township."

"We have a lot to be proud of, people," started Leonard, as he stood up and placed his hands on the table. "Like a phoenix, we have risen from the ashes. Miller's Ferry is not only back on the map, but now we're the town everybody wants to move to. It may have taken almost 200 years, but we have finally realized Heinrich Putzkammer's dream that 'all roads will lead to Pissquatta.' But there is trouble, good people," he continued, projecting his voice into both rooms of the restaurant. "Storm clouds gather on the horizon, a threat to everything for which we have worked and fought so hard. The county is trying to ram a landfill down our throats."

Around the room could be heard gasps of astonishment at this news.

"That's right, a landfill," he continued, "a mountain of garbage in our back yards. I, for one, simply won't stand still for it. How about you?"

The astonishment was quickly replaced with building anger.

"Since our forefathers first settled this land, we have been responsible stewards, each generation passing down to the next the wondrous beauty of our precious streams, our fertile fields, and the warmth of our people. Our battle isn't over. No, it has only begun. We shall fight the good fight to save our town and our way of life. I want you all to engage in petitions, along with a campaign of phone calls and letters to anyone who will listen. When you leave here today, I want you to spread the word and mobilize our Minute Men."

"Viva Viagra!" shouted someone from the main dining room.

Leonard's head sunk with the responding chuckles. "Damn it!" he boomed, pounding his fists on the table and seizing everybody's rapt attention. "No more speeches. Let me put it in a way you can all relate. Whatever your house appraises for today will only be a memory once that landfill goes in. Really, who wants to buy a house next to a dump? My voice is not going to be enough. If this town is to be heard, we all have to stand up and roar like I am doing right now!" Leonard sat back down at a table that was now in a more somber mood than before.

Beatrice placed a reassuring hand on his knee and kissed his cheek.

Mike leaned over and whispered in his ear, "Wow! I really need to come down here more often."

Leonard sat in his office in thoughtful contemplation. He felt the breakfast speech, his rallying of the troops, should have sufficiently motivated the people to defend the value of their homes, and with his last round of phone calls to friends and connections in the city, he had gone about as far he could. He knew as he sat back in his swivel chair that there was a flurry of phone calls and emails circulating the city, trying to muster the necessary interest and capital to make something happen. If he were a betting man, this would have been too much of a long shot to put money on, but he had been lucky in the past. His mind raced, generating and discarding any idea that might salvage his current situation, but always he came back to where he started.

The moment was suddenly broken by the sound of yelling in Lori's outer office, followed by his door being kicked in by Ned Fischer.

"Leonard, you son of a bitch!"

"Ned, what is this?"

"Why, I ought to pull you over that desk and kick your ass! Do you have any idea what you've done?"

"Ned, I have no idea. What's wrong?"

"That lynch mob you've stirred up in town, that's what's wrong!"

"Nobody was told it was your land, Ned! I purposely kept that back."

"Like anyone can keep a secret in this town! Hell, you might as well have put it on the evening news. You wouldn't believe the phone calls I've been getting, scaring my wife to death. How dare you!"

"Ned, please have a seat."

"What I got to say, I can say standing up. The deal is off. I'm signing the papers tomorrow at noon, and the landfill is going in."

"Alright! You've had your say, and now you're going to hear me out. You say you owe this town nothing, and I say that's bullshit. *You* are this town, along with everyone else you're brushing off to the side. You were the best wide receiver in high school- remember? Remember how the town turned out to cheer you on every Friday night? This town gave you your wife of forty-five years. This town raised your kids in our churches and in our schools. This town mortgaged your land, and this town has been by your side through all of your successes and failures. Do you really believe you owe this town nothing? What did you expect people would do after this kind of betrayal? You're worried about a few nasty phone calls, when the mob might have actually lynched you for what you're about to do!"

Ned chewed on Leonard's reprisal through gritted teeth and clenched fists, slowly losing the steam he had rolled in on. "Damn it, Len, they threatened me and Loretta," he replied at length, sitting in the chair in front of Leonard's desk. "Do you have any idea how scared she is right now? I know I ain't real popular with folks these days, but they threatened to shoot us."

"Ned, the crazy few don't speak for the rest of us."

"That may be, but I have a new interest to look after, so I'm signing tomorrow at noon and getting the heck outta Dodge. Look… I know it's a long shot, but if by some miracle you can match the offer by then, I'll give you first rights."

"You know we can't do that."

"I'm sorry, Len, but I'm done. Miller's Ferry isn't safe for us anymore, and I gotta get outta here while I can."

"Here's to Miller's Ferry! Long may she stink like trash!" said Leonard, holding up a glass of scotch in Itchy's office.

"I ain't a-drinking to that."

"Then what are you drinking to?"

"To surviving."

"That ain't enough for me, Itch."

"Did I ever tell about when I lost my arm, Leonard?"

"Yeah. You said you lost it working on a barge."

"That's right. A cable coupling busted loose on one of the barges, smashing it to pieces right below the shoulder. The force knocked me back and over the side between the two barges that were separating. They sprung apart as far as they could and sprung back with me in between. The whole thing happened so dern fast that no one could get to me in time. By the time they found me and managed to fish me out, I was more dead than alive. The one moment of consciousness I had at the hospital was to hear a doctor feller say it'd be a miracle if I lived."

"I had no idea it was that bad. I mean, you just showed back up here one day without an arm and a vague story of how you lost it."

"I really don't like to dwell on it much. Truth be told, it was a miracle I even survived. Now, I don't hold no stock in church, but I do believe the man upstairs was looking after me. Sinner that I am, I still can't figger that'n out. But needless to say, here I am. I survived. Sometimes, Len, you just have to pick up those pieces from your broken day and make do the best you can. This town will survive, and it will go on long after you and I have passed."

"Thank you, Itch. I think I needed to hear that."

"Yes, you did, but I have one more thing to add. Like I said, I believe in miracles. Hell, I'm living proof of one. Now, old Itchy Jackson's got one more card up his sleeve, so don't you go giving up on hope completely."

"What are you up to, old man?"

"Well, let's just say I put a call out to the Cavalry, and I'm leaving it at that. But as for now, let's get good and drunk and try our hand at some eight-ball."

CHAPTER TWENTY ONE

It was late in the morning at the Lucky Chance Ranch. The sun already had a good start on its transit across the sky and was now finishing with its daily task of drying up the remnants of the morning dew. A thin layer of dust hung over the dirt road leading up to the compound of buildings after the ranch pickup truck rattled and rolled over it up the bunkhouse. Angelo hopped from the cab and threw the door shut behind him. He strode across to the bunkhouse and stepped inside.

Bob was seated on the edge of his bunk, staring at a knothole in the worn pine plank flooring.

Angelo smiled and took a seat on the edge of his own bunk across from Bob. "What are we going to do today, Bob? Mend the fence on the back twenty?"

"Nope."

"Nope?"

"Nope."

"Some of the horses need to be shod. Are we going to do that?"

"Nope."

"Nope? What are you going to do today, Bob?"

Bob rose from his bunk and smoothed down his blue jeans. His boots struck solidly, and his spurs rattled as he walked across the cabin to a worn clothes chest. From within the chest, he withdrew his trusty six-shooters and belt, and then fastened them about his waist. He turned on a heel as he adjusted the belt to better hang on his hips, and then removed his favorite black Stetson from its hook on the wall and squared it on his head. "I have to go save the town."

"I see. There could be trouble, Bob. You think I should come along?"

"We'll saddle up the Arabians. Come on, partner. Let's ride."

The lawn outside of Ned Fischer's house had turned into a parking lot by eleven thirty. Ned's aged truck was surrounded by a small fleet of Escalades and BMWs, the preferred vehicles of the modern developer and his team of attorneys. They impatiently paced in small groups while Ned awaited the hour of noon before signing over his land on the hood of his truck.

The arrival of Leonard's pickup was a welcome distraction to Ned but a bothersome nuisance to everybody else. Its long approach down Ned's driveway was heralded by the metallic sound of grinds, bangs, and dings from the vehicle as it struggled over the worn road. At length, it found an open space amidst the shiny new vehicles, coughing, pinging, and shaking to a faltering stop after the engine had been turned off.

Ned looked over hopefully as Leonard emerged from the cab, but the face the defeated mayor bore betrayed the news he was about to deliver. Leonard brushed past the developers, rudely shouldering one that refused to get out of his way, and found Ned standing next to the front bumper of his own truck.

"Tell me you have something, Leonard, anything... and I'll stop this right now."

"I wish you'd reconsider, Ned, but I understand your reasons. I tried. God knows I tried, but I have nothing."

"Is it a matter of time? Even if all I have is a good-faith agreement and a down payment, I'll stop it right now."

"The fact is, Ned, this land is worth more to them than it will ever be to anyone else. Even if I had more time, I don't think we could ever match their price. I guess we'll just have to try to fight them in the courts."

"So that's it?" said Ned with all hope for a resolution lost.

"That's it," replied Leonard without any hope at all.

Ned saw in Leonard's face what was left for him to do. He held out his hand for the mayor to take. "I only hope that someday, you'll forgive me."

"Don't sweat it, Ned," he replied, taking the hand in his own firm grip. "Enjoy the rest of your life. You deserve it."

As the two men reconciled, several of the developers were gathering together, pointing off across a field left to fallow. Trailed by a cloud of dust were two riders on beautiful black Arabian horses, approaching at a full gallop. Curious, Ned and Leonard walked over next to the group to better see who was riding with such urgency.

"Len, who is that?" asked Ned.

"I don't know. Perhaps it's the Cavalry."

"Wait a minute! That's Belt Buckle Bob. What is that fool up to?"

"Who is that?" demanded one of the developers.

"Oh, his name is Bob. He's something of a village idiot."

"He's wearing guns."

"He's harmless," said Leonard. "He likes to think he's a cowboy."

The pair rode up to the group, and Bob and Angelo immediately dismounted. Angelo took the reins of both horses, while Bob walked directly over to Ned Fischer.

"Bob, what are you doing here?" asked Ned.

"Mr. Fischer, I'd like to introduce myself. My name is Robert Chance of the Lucky Chance Ranch, and I understand you have some land to sell. I want to buy it."

"Is this some kind of joke?"

"I assure you, sir, this is no joke. My attorney over there is Angelo DiSalvo, whom I believe some of those gentlemen should know by reputation," he continued, turning to the attorneys.

Three of the lawyers within the group of suits began talking in hoarse whispers, with the words "My God! It's really him!" reaching the ears of all involved. Angelo smiled and tilted his head back in a gesture of greeting.

"Mr. Fischer, I've brought a certified check in the amount of $850,000.01 as a counter offer." Bob removed an envelope folded in half from the pocket of his denim jacket and handed it over to Ned Fischer.

Ned took it, opened the flap, and looked inside to verify the contents. "I don't know, Len. It looks real."

Leonard looked at the check and then at Ned. "It is real. A friend of mine recently asked me not to give up on miracles. Is this one good enough for you?"

"We'll go higher," said one of the lawyers to Ned as he forced his way through the crowd. "Give us a chance to counter offer."

"I don't think you want to do that, mister," said Bob, placing himself between Ned and the lawyer. "Folks in town are already gearing up for a fight. I have more money than all of you put you together to help fight that fight, along with a lawyer who knows how to kick ass and take names to boot."

While the two tried to stare one another down, Ned eased around Bob. "That's alright, son, I can take it from here. I am very thankful for your generous offer, Mr. Lipschomb, but I have reconsidered my position. I'm sure you are prepared to offer me more money, but this is enough for me. I'm selling the property to Belt Buckle Bob Chance."

The developers wasted no time pursuing a reward they had no chance of attaining. They picked up their briefcases and started en masse to their shiny fleet of vehicles.

"Gentlemen!" Bob cried out after them.

They stopped and turned around.

"No one has to leave here empty handed. I want to buy out your land surrounding my property. Now that it's worthless to you, I'll give you what you paid, which I think you'll have to agree is more than generous. Just get a hold of my lawyer out at the Lucky Chance Ranch if you want to deal."

"Bob, I feel like I'm meeting you for the first time," said Leonard, walking over to shake his hand. "I never even knew you had a last name, and I probably still wouldn't have connected it to your ranch if I did."

"That's just the way I like it, Mr. Mayor. After we conclude our business today, I trust you will both forget it."

"Belt Buckle Bob sits fine with me. So, what are you going to do with the land, Bob?"

"We'll go ahead with the industrial park as planned, and I will cover all the costs associated with site development."

"That's what I would call a miracle. I already have five of the lots filled, I'm sure the last two will come soon enough."

"They already have. I'm putting up the venture capital for fuel cell technology. The group I'm financing has some big plans, and we'll need the square footage."

"That's quite ambitious for a karaoke-singing cowboy."

"Well, old Angelo over there, along with our mutual one-armed pool-hustlin' friend, did a pretty good job of convincing me into diversifying my portfolio."

"What about all that land surrounding the park?"

Bob's face spread into a big smile. "I've always wanted to try cattle. Hell, what else is a cowboy to do in his spare time?"

CHAPTER TWENTY TWO

The benefactor behind the purchase of Ned's property was as much a source of relief for the citizens of Miller's ferry as he was a source of mystery. It was a common topic of speculation in all of Leonard's pulse points, but true to his word, he never divulged the identity of the man behind the curtain. Some had even gone to great lengths to satisfy their curiosity by researching public records, but they always came back to a paper corporation mired down in even murkier mystery. In time, the novelty gave way to complacency once ground broke on the new industrial park. As the buildings went up and the doors opened for business, the magician behind the miracle was all but forgotten. The new park invited many of the town residents to work, which they thankfully accepted.

Also new to the landscape was the B&A Cattle Ranch that spread out through pastureland surrounding the industrial park. When not attending to the needs of the Lucky Chance Ranch, Bob and Angelo on horseback was a common site as they tended to the herd. On some nights, the two could be observed from the road nearby, lounging by an open fire, propped on their bedrolls, looking at the star-filled sky, and living the dream of honest-to-goodness cowboys.

But on this particular Saturday afternoon, Belt Buckle Bob stood on his favorite street corner, assuming his classic pose, replete in all the details of his persona, down to the hand-rolled cigarette dangling from his lips. With the sun on its final decent, the light shone brilliantly on him and gleamed off his huge rodeo belt buckle.

The quiet of the moment was broken by the sound of Leonard's truck as it approached almost a block away. Having recently lost its muffler, it was now even more of an obscenity to anyone who beheld it. The truck rolled to a stop in front of Bob, and Leonard leaned across the seat to roll down the passenger-side window. "How ya doing, Bob?" asked Leonard.

Bob shifted his weight to his other leg and slowly replied, "Good."

"You heading up to the saloon tonight?"

"Yep."

"You gonna sing some karaoke?"

"Yep."

"Good. I might stop up later on. You think you could save a duet for me?"

"Nope. Solo tonight."

"Sure, sure. A least let me buy you a beer."

"Yep."

"Great. I'll see you later then?"

"Yep."

Leonard drove up to Itchy's Billiard Parlor in time to see the last of the street-front parking spaces taken by a carload of Goth kids, so instead he pulled around into the parking lot out back. Within the next couple of hours, this lot also would be filled with the vehicles of Itchy's patrons, but for now, he had the choice of spots and settled his truck into the one closest to the rear entrance.

Since Itchy had bought a liquor license, his humble beatnik hideaway had evolved into one of the hottest hangouts in the county. Leonard strolled past the new bar, giving his regards to Angelina on his way to the pool tables, where Amanda and her husband were in fierce competition in a game of snooker. Their happiness was evident in every move they made together, a direct result of their own recent successes. John had finally found gainful employment in the new engineering firm in the industrial park. Amanda still dabbled in spectral investigations, but these days, she was busily promoting her new haunted romance novel. After exchanging his greetings with them, Leonard headed out towards the bandstand and tables.

Itchy was sitting and chatting at a table with Eddie and his partner James.

Leonard took up an empty seat next to Eddie. "How is everyone tonight?"

"Fine, Mr. Mayor. And yourself?" replied Eddie.

"Fine, fine. Say, I hear you have political aspirations in the next election."

"That's a fact. I hope there are no hard feelings."

"Never. I think you'd make a fine mayor. I'll put up a good fight, but I won't regret it if I lose. I think it may be time to turn the reins over to someone younger."

"Thanks. That means a lot to me. You know James is running for the school board?"

"He has my vote and my full endorsement."

"Thanks, Mr. Mayor. I appreciate that," replied James.

Leonard dismissed the notion with a wave of his hand. "I think you'll do a fine job. Itchy, I was hoping you might want to share a glass or two of the good stuff."

"Sure, Len. Why don't you come on in the back? There's something I want to show you."

Walking into the back office, Leonard was met by the return of Itchy's old desk, complete with the detritus in which it was accustomed to being adorned.

"Will you look at that? It's like seeing an old friend again. What did you do with the new one?"

"Oh, it's in the office at home. Angelina uses it mostly— already has our wedding photos spread along the edge of it."

"That's great. How is the catering business doing?"

"Swell. In fact, the kitchen here is getting too small for her. I haven't told her yet, but I'm fixing to set her up in a brand new restaurant. We'll still serve the same menu here, but with the new place, she'll have the space to grow as much as she wants."

"My, my, how quickly the times are a-changing. If it weren't for our little sojourns, I wouldn't have a clue as to what's going on."

After filling two coffee cups with the good stuff and giving one to Leonard, who sat comfortably ensconced in his familiar place on the old sofa, Itchy settled down into his favorite oak office chair and kicked his feet up onto their worn spot at the edge of the desk.

"Say, Itchy, what happened to that plaque you used to have up their above your head?"

"The broken pool cue? Oh, I took it down. A respectable businessman shouldn't be a braggin' over cracking a stick on someone's head, even if the other guy did have a knife."

"I'm sure that's a story unto itself."

"Surely is, but I'll have to get good and drunk before I'll tell it. So you think ol' Eddie out there has a shot at your office?"

"No... not unless I gave it to him."

"Strange answer. Are you a-ruminatin' something over there?"

"I sure am, but don't tell anybody. Personally, I think he'd do a great job, but I could win without even showing up. Now, if I were to cede too early, that might open up the door to any

Tom, Dick, or Harry, but if I were to wait until the night before the election... well, I think his chances might improve."

"Really? You retirin'? I think it's a sign of the coming of the apocalypse."

"My work here is done Itch, and I was telling the truth out there about someone younger taking over. This town has a real chance of becoming something great, and it will take some forward-thinking leadership to take us there."

"Ain't you something? So, what do you plan to do with your time now?"

"That's an easy one. I'm gonna marry Bea and take an extended honeymoon."

"You-are-kidding-me! Well, Goddamn, you are pulling some rabbits outta yer hat tonight! Have you asked her yet?"

"No. I plan to take her down to Louisville next week and ask her there."

"Oh, I love Louisville. Are you staying at The Brown?"

"Of course, and I've made reservations at the Oak Room, where I plan to pop the question."

"Fantastic. And what of this extended honeymoon?"

"I've got a fair amount in my savings, so I plan to take her on a three-month tour of the museums of Europe."

"Man, you're pushing all the right buttons with that woman."

"I'd like to think so."

"So, you hanging around here tonight? We have a great band coming in."

"Sorry, Itch, but I'll have to take a pass. Bea and I have dinner plans with Mike and Eunice."

"That's just as well. If"n Angelina and me can ever tear ourselves away from making money, I'd like to jump in on some of them dinner plans."

"Let us know. We'll make some space at the table for you. Say, Belt Buckle Bob is singing later tonight at the Stumble Inn."

"Is he now? Maybe I can slip out a little early fer a nightcap."

"I'll be buying if you do."

"You gonna do a duet with him again?"

"Nah. He said he wants to sing solo tonight."

"I wish he'd get Angelo to come out more. He has a beautiful voice."

"Is that so? Hard to figure, since neither one of them says much."

"In their case, they let their actions do that for 'em. I've known about them two since the Lucky Chance first opened up. The way I figger it, they know everything what needs knowin' about one another. After that, there ain't much worth saying."

"Are they... um... a couple?"

"No more than you and me. Angelo's got him some action in the city when he needs a little female companionship, and Bob... well, he's holding out for the right woman to come along. He's afraid if everyone knows his little secret, he'll never find the one woman who will love him for his eccentricities. No, Len, they're just two fellers who enjoy each other's company."

"This town has seen the most unlikely of heroes these past two years."

"And one of 'em is sitting on my sofa."

"It's hard for me to see myself in that light."

"That, my friend, is all part of being a hero, now isn't it? As the mayor of the most haunted town in America, I'd say you earned it all fair and square."

"And so it is. To the heroes of Miller's Ferry!"

"I'll drink to that!"

The night ran wild in Itchy's Billiard Parlor. He sent Angelina home early, and opted to close up by himself. He would have to take a pass on Bob's crooning, but there would be other nights. After escorting the last of the last-call customers out the door, he flipped the 'closed' sign and locked up. He would save the cleanup for the morning, but tend to the till before leaving. He took the cash register drawer back into his office and placed it on the desk before stooping down to open up the stout cast-iron safe behind his desk.

The tumblers of the lock clicked while he spun the combination dial, and as he swung the big brass handle to open up the door, he heard a resounding thwack of pool balls coming from the parlor. Itchy was old school and devoutly believed in the right to bear to arms. After removing his Smith and Wesson from the desk drawer, he quietly crept out to the billiard hall. The sound of a cue ball smacking another ball into a side pocket echoed off the walls, but the source remained a mystery, for he was alone amidst the tables.

At the far table, he watched in disbelief as a cue ball traversed the felt, sinking a ball in the corner pocket, only to scratch.

"Damn!" came a voice out of a shadow that slowly materialized behind the table. To Itchy's amazement, the shadow slowly took the form of flesh and clothes, until it beheld a very recognizable man.

"I know you! Lloyd's Tavern, 1967. You were my first."

"And you were my last. Still can't believe you beat the manslaughter charges."

"Maybe it was the twenty-seven stitches you left in my side what helped my case," Itchy replied, sticking the revolver in his waistband.

"I don't begrudge you none, Itchy. It was a fair fight, even if you did start it."

"I started it? You forget how you scratched on the eight-ball and refused to settle your bets!"

"Oh… that's right. No hard feelings then?"

"That depends. You come here to pay up?"

"I come for a rematch."

"Really? And what makes you think you have a chance?" he asked the specter, walking over to the table.

"You ain't got but one arm now, and I've had plenty of time to practice."

"Humph. Is that right? Say, what made you come back after all these years?"

"You took the plaque down."

"I felt kind of guilty over'n it."

"Don't! You were the only one what kept my memory alive. You might not know it, but I wasn't a very likable guy when I was alive."

"No kiddin'! Hmm… alrighty then. I'll rack 'em, and you can break."

"Let's play some pool, Itch."

I wish to thank Autumn for making the book shine,
Kate for tying up the loose ends, and my port & cigar buddy
David for helping me find Itchy.